A MAN EATER IN KASAN KADU

BALAMURUGAN K A

INDIA • SINGAPORE • MALAYSIA

ISBN 979-8-89186-991-2

Pencil art by Gayathri Balamurugan

This book is a humble tribute to the remarkable legacies of Jim Corbett and Kenneth Anderson, who were not only great hunters but also gifted writers. The pages of this fictional book serve as a testament to the profound impact their works have had on readers around the world.

CONTENTS

ACKNOWLEDGEMENTS

First and foremost, I would like to start the acknowledgement by expressing my earnest gratitude to the Almighty for his abundant grace in both my career and my life.

My family's constant support has left me tremendously indebted. My lovable parents, Kathirvel and Amutha, have always been a constant source of strength. I would like to express my gratitude to my brothers Velusamy and Karthick for their persistent moral support, vital motivation, and guidance.

I am grateful to my wife, Malathi, for her steadfast support and tolerance during the entire book-writing process. Her encouragement and helpful constructive feedback were extremely valuable; I could not have completed this venture without her. I would like to thank my lovely daughters, Gayathri and Kiruthika, for their constant backing at this particular juncture. A special thanks to my daughter Gayathri for her pencil art of the tiger.

Dr. A. Velusamy, my brother, made a significant contribution to this book, for which I am exceedingly grateful. From the start of this book to its final stage, he has helped me to hone my ideas and concepts by offering advice and encouragement. He wrote a foreword to this book that is quite outstanding. In addition, I want to express my sincere gratitude to him for his meticulous editing and the execution of the piece of literature.

I offer a debt of gratitude to the Textbook team, coordinated by Vimala Devi, and my friends, as well as teammates Sathyaraj, Rajeshpandi, Uthirapathi, Vairamuthu, and Aruna, for their invaluable assistance in helping me realise my literary potential.

My friend, Uthirapathi, has been my greatest source of inspiration and has immensely improved the quality and clarity of the content. Also, I acknowledge the assistance of my friends Ponkarthik, Balaji Karthick, and Meenakshi, as their efforts have greatly improved the writing of the book.

– K A Balamurugan

PREFACE

I was fortunate enough to become acquainted with the writings of the well-known hunter and author Jim Corbett during my time in school. I read about his near-death experience with a snake in the restroom and his valiant killing of a man-eating tiger while holding a rifle in one hand and two fragile bird eggs in the other in one of my English textbooks. I eventually learned that the man-eating tiger was *the Chowgarh Tiger* from the book *The Maneaters of Kumaon,* and the snake encounter was from his book *My India*, chapter titled *Life at Mokameh Ghat*, despite the fact that I cannot remember the actual title of these lessons.

I came across the book *The Man-Eating Leopard of Rudraprayag* when I was a college student, exploring at a bookstore in Thanjavur. My curiosity about Jim Corbett's writing was aroused by that book, which I had not known about. The storyline of that book never fails to enthral me, no matter how many times I've read it. The writing and hunting prowess of Jim Corbett are portrayed in his books. I looked in local bookshops, but I was unable to locate his other works. But thanks to the internet and e-commerce, I was able to buy his collections of works, including *The Jim Corbett Omnibus Vols. 1 and 2*, as well as other books that I truly enjoyed reading.

When I browsed the remarks on an Indian e-commerce website concerning Jim Corbett's books, I came across the name of renowned hunter and author Kenneth Anderson. Inspired by his writings, I looked for more of his books and eventually bought *The Kenneth Anderson Omnibus Vols. 1, 2, and 3* in addition to other volumes. It is difficult to go on an exciting and hunting-filled real-world expedition, but these books took me there.

I had a habit of narrating these stories to my wife, Malathi, and on one occasion, she asked me what would happen if there was a man-eating tiger in our village. Her inquiry ignited my imagination, and I started recording the events that came to my mind by using my cell phone. Finally, I ended up writing this fictional novel using the knowledge I gained from these works.

FOREWORD

Dr. VELUSAMY. A,
Assistant Professor of English,
Government Arts College,
Ariyalur – 621 713.

First of all, a tiger in the Ariyalur district is intriguing because I am from the same area. I had an incredible experience turning the pages of this book and thoroughly enjoyed reading it.

An acknowledgement of rural wildlife in a brief opening that repeatedly occurs in subsequent chapters demonstrates the author's deep affection for the landscape as well as the ability to take readers on an unforgettable journey.

When we pick up a book written by one of our favourite authors, a wave of happiness and nostalgia spreads over us. My experience with "The Man-eater in Kasan Kadu" by K A Balamurugan was quite the same. The writer was not just a man haunted by the image of the tiger that slaughtered people or lifted cattle. The tradition included a patriarchal perspective on occupants and cattle grazers.

This book features a narrative that draws readers in and keeps them turning pages. The story is brimming with a lot of characters. The narration is lively and captivating. Assuming these events are true, we must respect the willingness to make the excruciating efforts necessary to track down the man-eaters, sometimes putting the poacher's own life in danger.

The writer additionally notes that the tiger does not hunt humans and that in practice it does so because of external factors rather than a natural attraction for human blood. His writing is so concise that it appears effortless to turn the pages, and the book leaves us in wonderment.

I would recommend this book to anyone who enjoys exploring the great outdoors and animals, as it goes beyond simple facts and offers readers an exciting journey through Ariyalur District's forests.

Dr. A. VELUSAMY

ONE

Sethupalayam, a remote village on the fringes of the Sathya Mangalam tiger reserve, was damp from the mist and dew of *Pin Pani Kalam,* the last of six seasons in Tamil Nadu, which falls in late February and early March. This season brings the last mist and dew before the *Ila-venil Kalam* falls in, followed by *Mudhu-venil Kalam* (summer in Tamil Nadu). On one such misty morning in the final days of February 2023, before dawn broke out, Arivalagan set out to the tiger reserve to trap wild rabbits with *muyal kanni.* Being a skilled tracker and hunter, he resorted to poaching, sneaking into the tiger reserve to trap small wild animals, collect honey, and sell them on the black market.

The *Muyal kanni* that Arivalagan carried was a homemade snare made using steel binding wires known as *kattukambi.* Arivalagan made multiple nooses with steel bind wire and tied them all in a row with a long, stretched wire. He looked for a place in the forest where rabbits frequently roamed and tied the snare. Any rabbit that crossed the noose would be caught. He carried four such muyal kanni and started walking north towards the forest. His plan was to tie each snare in four different locations, increasing his chance of catching at least one rabbit. He started early in the morning from his village to track the rabbits. He knew that if the cattle started grazing in the area, they would disturb the tracks of the rabbits.

As he was familiar with the forest, he knew precisely where the rabbits tended to roam. While walking along the edge of the forest, he kept his eyes peeled for any signs of rabbit tracks. Suddenly, he stumbled upon a spot where the soil was stained with a dark red colour. Upon closer inspection, he realised that it was blood. Glancing around, he saw more blood trails leading from the village to the tiger reserve, running from south to north. He felt a rush of excitement but also a sense of nervousness.

Based on his experience in the forest, he deduced that a tiger or a leopard had hunted and brought its prey into the reserve. The dried blood indicated that the kill had taken place the previous evening. He concluded that the victim was most likely a solitary cow grazing away from the herd or far from the herders' sight. The blood trail on his left led to the place where the animal was killed, and the right, towards the forest, led to where the predator ate its prey. Although he wanted to go right, he decided to go left first to identify the animal he was tracking. He didn't want to risk walking towards the predator without knowing what he was facing. He walked slowly, carefully examining the ground for any clues. After a few minutes of tracking, he found what he was looking for—a pug mark of a tiger.

As the terrain he was moving through was rough, he could not find any pug marks until he spotted one imprinted on the soft soil. His expert eyes quickly recognised it as the left fore paw of the tiger, with one large circle and four smaller ones on top. A smile spread across his face as he realised that the tiger, which had been reported to have been killing cattle around the villages twenty kilometres away, had made its way to their side of the jungle.

As soon as Arivalagan confirmed that he was tracking a tiger, he turned around and began heading towards the kill, following the blood trail. Since the terrain was hard and covered with grass, he could not see the tiger's foot prints; they were only visible in the soft soil. He concluded that the tiger had killed a young cow, as there were no signs of the animal being dragged. The tiger seemed to have carried its kill without difficulty, and so there was no drag mark. The kill was not a burden since the tiger had not dropped the kill to change the hold. The tiger quickly carried it off leaving, only a trail of blood. The blood trail had been visible until it entered the dense forest area. The forest was thick with trees, and the ground was covered in grasses and bushes. The landscape ahead of him was covered with tall bushes and a few trees.

His senses warned him of the possible danger ahead of him, so he stopped for a moment to consider his next move. Tracking a normal tiger is generally less risky as they try to avoid conflict with humans. However, they can still be dangerous, especially, when they are with the cubs, during mating season and when it is busy eating. So, he should be very cautious when approaching the tiger. He didn't want to step on a tiger resting after a good meal. So, he looked around and decided to climb on a peepal tree with branches spread all over the bushes. He reached the foot of the tree, dropped the snare and the bags, and started climbing the tree without making any noise.

A snap from a twig would alert the tiger; either it would come to check the source of it or it would be gone.

He climbed a branch that went high over the area he intended to scan. He reached the end of the branch and scanned the ground. He was a little disappointed that the tiger was not there. But he saw the kill, seventy feet away from the tree, of a half-grown bull; most of the ribs and the hind parts were eaten. There was a good portion of the bull left for another full meal. So, he decided to return late in the afternoon, sit on the same tree, and see the tiger. He climbed down, went straight to the kill, and checked the pug marks; it was a clean specimen of a pug mark left by a young male tiger in its prime. The tiger must have had a very peaceful meal. Then it lay down on the grass to rest and walked towards the reserve. Arivalagan collected the scattered dry branches, covered the remains of the bull to keep away the vultures, and walked home. On his way back to the village, he tied his *muyal kanni* in four spots where the rabbits tend to be.

Arivalagan came to the spot in the late afternoon. He was glad to see the cover on the kill untouched and that the tiger had not returned while he was away. But he had another problem: there were Karung Kurang, the black-footed gray langur everywhere. Every troop of these monkeys will have a watcher; the watcher monkey will reach a high branch and watch the surroundings for predators, and the other monkeys will go around and fill their stomachs. When the watcher finds a predator or any other danger, it will warn the troop. The other monkeys will alight the trees nearby for safety.

Presently, the watcher of the troop saw Arivalagan from his elevated post, and it gave a sharp warning call to the troop, announcing them about the intruder. A little chaos followed the alarm. The entire troop started crying in alarm;

the mothers hurriedly took their infants to safety, and the monkeys roaming around climbed high on the trees. It took nearly half an hour to get things settled. But still, the watcher kept his eyes on Arivalagan.

Arivalagan avoided eye contact with the watcher and went around with his work. He went to the kill and removed the branches he used to cover it. He stood between the legs of the bull, looked at the tree, and selected a branch that gave him a perfect hide. Then he returned to the tree and climbed the branch he selected with a good hide. The watcher was watching him all the time. At around 4:30 p.m., the monkeys moved on towards the reserve. By the time the darkness fell, the monkeys had settled in the trees closer to the reserve, and their clattering could be heard clearly.

The branch that Arivalagan selected gave him proper concealment, so he relaxed and started to wait. He was relieved that the monkeys had left the area, as they would have alerted the tiger of his presence. However, their absence could also be a disadvantage, as they would have warned him of the tiger's approach. He started to wait for the arrival of the tiger. He wanted to confirm that the tiger was interested in a second meal. When almost the darkness had set in, he heard the monkey's sharp, terrified alarm call for a couple of minutes, and then a perfect silence fell in. The watcher of the troop had definitely seen a predator and was alerting his troop, and they stopped the cry once the tiger had moved away. And now it was clear that the tiger had crossed the troop and was moving towards the kill.

Anticipation was raised in Arivalagan's mind. He prayed that it would be the same tiger that killed the bull. The scenery around him disappeared into the darkness. But the moon and starlight gradually lit the surroundings, and the objects around him appeared as shadows. He sat still and waited for the tiger to come in. He knew the tiger would take time to check the surroundings before approaching the kill. Then, from time to time, he heard the sound of an animal moving among the bushes. After around half an hour, he heard the crushing sound of bones. A swift heat went through his body, and he started to sweat from the pores of his skin. His trembling hands moved the leaves that blocked his view, and he saw a young male tiger eating from the kill. Even his heart, experienced in the hazardous jungle, started pounding. The moonlight traced the coat of reddish orange with black stripes, and when the tiger turned around, he saw the faultless face of the tiger with glowing eyes that captivated his eyes. His mood altered from fear to thrill and excitement. Having contented himself, he sat back comfortably, for he couldn't climb down; any little noise would disturb the tiger, and it would learn that it should not return to any kill for a second meal. Then, it will be difficult to trap it, and the number of kills will increase. So, he decided to wait until the morning.

TWO

Arul and Viji arrived at the location provided to them, near Dharmapuri on the Salem-Bangalore highway. They parked their Mahindra Major on the side of the road, at a safe distance from the traffic. They had to wait for their contacts to arrive. Arul said, "Viji, message them that we've arrived and ask their current location. You can also track their live location." Arul then went down the road for a quick break while Viji checked his cell phone. A few moments later, Arul returned, and Viji informed him, "I've checked their live location; they are still fifteen kilometres away from us and moving slowly. I hope they'll be here in twenty minutes." Viji then took his turn to step away from the road. Arul leaned on the Jeep and stared at the moving vehicles. "This time, we should avoid Magesh," said Viji, walking to the jeep and leaning on the bonnet beside Arul. "He always drinks and doesn't take the situation seriously. Last time, he almost ruined everything in full boost."

"Who else do you suggest? Nowadays, all are drunkards," replied Arul.

"It's dangerous to take such a person for our job. The decision is up to you. However, I recommend we take Kolanji and Dhinesh instead."

"Kolanji lacks experience," replied Arul.

"We can teach Kolanji. But that drunkard never listens to us once the liquor is inside. He will make much fuss."

"Okay, we will take Kolanji, but he is your problem."

Arul wanted to end the conversation, so he took out his cell phone and watched video songs. Viji opened the back door of the Jeep and lay down on one of the two seats.

Arul was a tall man, standing at 6 feet, with a commanding look and dark skin. On the other hand, his friend and business partner, Viji, was slightly shorter but well-built, with a wheatish complexion. Both of them started their careers in the forest department. Arul was a veterinary doctor, and Viji was a sharpshooter. Together, they worked as a team in several forest regions and tiger reserves across India. Their job was to tranquillise and treat wounded animals. Arul was responsible for preparing tranquilliser darts, while Viji would shoot the wounded and sick animals. Once the animals were immobilised, Arul would treat them.

Everything was going smoothly until one day, poachers convinced them to join their trade. However, they were caught in the act and subsequently suspended. After that, they decided to take up poaching as a full-time job.

The next fifteen minutes passed at a snail's pace, and they had to endure a dreary wait. Eventually, Arul noticed a motorcycle approaching them from the opposite direction and thought it might be their contact. However, he wanted to verify it. "Viji, I think they are here." Arul pointed to the motorcycle. "You better check the live location," said Arul. Viji checked his phone and confirmed, "Yes, it's them."

confirmed Viji. He stepped out of the jeep and shut the back door while the motorcycle pulled up in front of them.

Arul dialled his contact's number, and the phone in the pocket of the pillion rider rang. The two men alighted from the motorcycle, made their way directly to Arul, and presented his phone to confirm the number. The person riding the motorcycle was tall and of average build. He walked away from the others and began looking at the road. The other man was stout and well-dressed. He handed a cloth bag to Arul and said, "Finish the work quickly. Call me when you're ready, and I will send the vehicle and other things."

"I'll call you when everything is ready," replied Arul. The man returned to the two-wheeler and said, "Let's go." They both got on the motorcycle and rode away in the same direction they came.

Arul turned to Viji and said, "Viji, call Arivalagan and let him know we're coming."They both got into the jeep and drove away.

Arul and Viji started looking for customers after Arivalagan told them that a tiger regularly comes out of the reserve and takes a toll on the cattle grazing on the outskirts of his village. Their contacts struck the deal, and they were paid in full. The name and the whereabouts of the customer were not disclosed to them. But they understood that the deal came from some people in higher positions in the government. Their part is to trap and transport the tiger safely to Pudukottai. They can walk away after handing the tiger to the person waiting in Pudukottai.

In the next two hours, Arul and Viji were in Arivalagan's village, Sethupalayam. They parked their jeep on the outskirts of the village. Arul stayed in the jeep, and Viji walked into the village to meet Arivalagan. After ten minutes, Viji and Arivalagan arrived to meet Arul. "Come, let's take a walk," suggested Arivalagan. The three walked silently along the road until Arivalagan questioned, "Are you sure the party is genuine?" Arul confirmed, "Yes, why do you doubt? We received half the payment in cash. Now it's our responsibility to finish the job." Arul asked, "Is your tiger still moving around the place?" Arivalagan replied, "If you have time, I will take you to the spot, and you can check for yourself." Arul agreed, saying, "We have all day. Moreover, we must get familiar with the area." Arivalagan began to walk into the forest. As they walked into the forest, they saw the cattle grazing in the green pastures and a few men looking after them. After a twenty-minute walk, they reached a spot where the density of the vegetation started to get thick.

Arivalagan led Arul and Viji to a spot and showed them the pugmarks of the tiger on the ground. Arul and Viji were excited. "This is three days old. Are there any new pugmarks?" asked Arul. He took out his cell phone and took photos of the pugmarks. He thoughtfully said, "Let us check the area for fresh ones." They all spread out and scanned the area. But they could not find any fresh pug marks; Arivalagan consoled them, "Don't worry, I have been tracking this tiger ever since I told you. It is a male tiger in its prime. It comes out to roam around and takes the cattle that graze near the forest. So far, it has killed around six cattle. I hope it will kill another one and give us a chance." "Can we tie a bait and sit over it?" asked Viji. Arivalagan rejected that idea: "No, it is dangerous. People will be watching us. I will let you know when it happens. You stay in Kattur. It will be easy for you to reach, and you better keep everything ready." "I saw many people moving around. What if they gather around after a kill? Won't they get suspicious of our activities?" Viji asked. Arivalagan said, "I have been following this tiger for about two months. Whenever the tiger kills a cow, the people in that area run away and dare not track it, fearing that if they disturb the tiger, it will intensify its kills. The people will inform the police and the forest department, but they will arrive the following day. And that gives us a whole night to finish the job without any interference. You better keep everything ready, and let's go now, concluded Arivalagan. They walked back, reached the Jeep, and drove off while Arivalagan walked to his village. Arul and Viji followed Arivalagan's instructions and arrived at Kattur. They found a place to stay, prepared all the equipment to trap a tiger, and started to wait.

On the third day after they met, Arivalagan received news that the tiger had killed a cow that was grazing away from the herd and dragged it near the reserve. Arivalagan arrived at the location and found it deserted; the herdsmen and cattle had fled in fear. The kill occurred a kilometre east of the previous one, so Arivalagan needed to trace it first. The owner of the cow would inform the appropriate authorities. Since the kill occurred in the afternoon, there was a chance that officials might visit the spot late in the evening before sunset. However, they could be afraid to track the dead cow at dusk and might choose to investigate the following day. Arivalagan had to wait and see what would happen next. He called Arul to inform him about the kill and asked him to wait on the outskirts of the village.

Arivalagan waited in the spot where the kill occurred for about two hours, but there was no activity. He understood that they had the whole night at their disposal. He could also see that the tiger had grown bolder, attacking the cattle in daylight. So, he carefully tracked and spotted the kill. A good portion of the cow was left out for a second meal. So, he covered the left out of the kill with branches of the plants and then called Arul and Viji and told them the location of the kill.

Arul and Viji drove in after fifteen minutes. They brought Dhinesh and Kolanji along with them. The five visited the spot carrying everything needed for the night. In the meantime, three local hunters, whom Arivalagan called to assist them, arrived. They first arrived at the spot where the tiger had killed its prey. Arivalagan pointed out the pug marks and the blood trail that led towards the reserve. They also found the spot where the tiger had been waiting for the right moment to attack the cow. The grass in this spot still bore the impression left by the tiger. They continued their search for the spot where the remains of the cow were lying. The blood trail was thin initially but turned into a pool in one place, where the tiger dropped the cow and changed its grip. From there, the blood trail was thick. They suspected that the tiger could still be nearby, so they proceeded with caution.

After walking for fifteen minutes, Arivalagan led them to the spot and gestured for them to proceed cautiously. They spread out to survey the area and carefully approached the animal carcass. Upon examination, Arul and Viji were satisfied that it was a tiger's kill. The neck was broken, and there were pugmarks all around the place. Arul verified if they were the same pugmarks that Arivalagan showed them three days ago. Then they checked the kill: the abdomen of the cow was open, the rib was half eaten, and the front and hind thigh were also eaten. They saw the inside of the cow lying in the distance. It was also a clear indication that a tiger made the kill. If it had been a leopard, the kill would be messy because it would not remove the internal organs. Now, they had to carefully select a tree to construct a paran.

A paran is a small hideout built on a tree or four stout poles. With proper concealment, the hunters sat on it, waited for their targets, and then shot them. An easy paran was constructed using a string cot. In recent days, tree stands have also been used. In the present case, they are after a tiger, so they resorted to a conventional paran. There were many trees; Arivalagan chose a tall peepal tree thirty feet away from the kill. Arul accepted it, and Arivalagan, Dhinesh, and Kolanji, with the help of the local hunters, started constructing the paran. Arul and Viji went around the border of the reserve. They decided to construct another paran on a tree, almost on the fringe of the forest, where they found the pug mark of the same tiger. If they miss it near the kill, this would help them secure the tiger. So, they returned to the spot and dispatched two local hunters and Viji to construct the second paran. They used small string cots for this purpose. After hanging the paran, they concealed the paran carefully and double-checked them. The local hunters that Arivalagan used were highly experienced in poaching, so their paran and concealment were so natural.

Arul and Kolanji climbed the paran near the kill, while Viji and Dhinesh climbed the one near the reserve. After they settled in the paran, their companions removed the branches spread on the left out of the kill and left the place carrying their tools and talking loudly, proclaiming to the tiger that they had finished working and had left the place. They don't want to take chances if the tiger happens to be watching them from its hide.

Arul and Viji had already advised their companions about sitting on a paran. Their hide was very safe, so they could make slight moves but not make sounds. They effortlessly blended in with the leaves as they wore the camouflage dresses of the forest department. Unlike the previous generation of hunters, Arul and Viji had the latest hunting equipment. They were equipped with imported or smuggled dart guns with a range of two hundred feet, fitted with thermal and night vision scopes. They were also assisted by thermal and night vision binoculars. They had a.12-bore double-barrel hunting gun for their safety. They were fully equipped to sit out the whole night. They started to wait for the tiger.

The time moved slowly; nothing exciting happened in the afternoon. The sunset was honoured by the singing of the birds that reached their homes. Gradually, the forest and its surroundings started to set in for the night. The birds went silent to give way to the crickets, which started chirping in different tones. Everywhere, it was pitch-black, and mosquitoes started buzzing around. Arul started to look through the hole left for peeping. He used his thermal imaging binoculars to check the kill and the surroundings. He looked at his watch. At almost seven, he warned Kolanji by touching his knee; 'no movement and no sound, sit still' was conveyed in it.

In the paran near the fringe of the reserve, Viji and Dhinesh waited with their equipment, Viji with a dart gun fitted with a scope and Dhinesh with the binoculars. Viji was facing the area, which was frequented by the tiger. Around half past seven, Dhinesh's binoculars picked up a reddish-yellow image. Gradually, the size grew, and it appeared to be a large animal. Dhinesh nudged the back of Viji. Viji turned around his gun slowly and looked into the scope. He could see the tiger slowly crossing them in thermal scope. He gave the alarm sound of a Karung Kurangu which was common in the area. The warning reached the ears of Arul. He got ready, quickly checked his dart rifle and scope, and came to a still, just listening to the night, the rustling sound of a dry leaf or the rolling of a stone, the brushing sound against a bush—anything that indicates the arrival of the tiger. He had to wait patiently, for the tiger wouldn't approach its kill deliberately. It will make several circles around the spot to check for other predators and then move in slowly.

Almost half an hour later, a sudden silence fell on the scene and indicated the arrival of a tiger. Arul heard a soft rustling sound. He tried to locate the sound. It came behind the tree where he was sitting. He doubted if his hide was compromised. After a few minutes, the sound came from the left side of the tree, then silence. Then, the sound came from the opposite direction, silent for a few minutes. Finally, he heard the cracking sound of bones from the kill. He slowly moved the rifle butt to his shoulder and saw through the scope. The tiger was lying between the legs of the remains of the cow and started eating the ribs of the cow. Arul, without further delay, fired the dart. The dart hit the tiger in the left shoulder; it was a tranquilliser. The tiger jumped in the air, growling, and then somersaulted and fell to the ground. Then it went around in circles, trying to bite off the dart, and, out of fear, started running in the opposite direction. Arul loaded a low-dose sedative dart in the gun and followed its movements through the scope and binoculars.

Meanwhile, Viji heard the sounds made by the tiger. He also removed the tranquilliser, loaded a sedative dart, and watched the surroundings with thermal imagers. After a few minutes, he spotted the tiger approaching his side, towards the reserve. But it was not coming towards his paran. So, he jumped down the paran, ran towards the spot where he guessed he could intercept the tiger, and took cover behind a tree. As the tiger approached, he fired the dart; this time, the tiger didn't growl. The tranquilliser had its effect. The tiger slowly entered the reserve and collapsed after a few minutes, running here and there.

Dhinesh and Kolanji were sent out to call in for help and to bring in the vehicle. Arul and Viji sat behind a tree nearby and watched the tiger. They grabbed a few stones and pelted the tiger. It let out a low growl but didn't move. They carefully approached the tiger and examined it. It was a perfect specimen of a young tiger. They waited for half an hour, and then Tata Yodha, an old ATM mobile cash-filling vehicle, came in. The old vehicle was not pleasing to Arul, but he had no other option because this vehicle could easily make it through any barriers. These vehicles are strong but lack the space to transport a tiger. It was a five-seater and had a big safe to load the package. The door to the package space was from the inside. The last seat of the five-seater had to be lifted to access the door. The back door was not provided, and only a small opening was given, which had to be opened from the inside. So, they hurriedly made passage in the back and wielded a door with a latch.

They had no time to waste. So, they swiftly loaded the tiger into the vehicle, and Arul noted that a padlock was needed for extra safety. Arul and Viji boarded the vehicle and checked on the tiger. While the others dismantled the paran, without wasting time, they started moving towards the village. Arul and Viji wore the uniforms used by security guards, and with their.12-bore guns, they looked perfectly like Mobile Cash Van guards. They reached the road and started to drive through the highway towards Trichy. Two Sumos escorted them in front and back within a five-minute distance. Dhinesh was driving the ATM cash vehicle, and then, after some time, Kolanji replaced him. They didn't stop anywhere.

At 3:00 AM, they stopped on a lonely village road to check on the tiger. Then they continued on the village road. Kolanji continued to drive the van. Arul felt he was driving fast and warned him, "Dai Kolanji, this is not a highway. Slow down the van. There will be a lot of curves and bends. Anything goes wrong, and we will end up in trouble." Kolanji slowed the van. The van continued on that lonely road.

The roads were chosen well in advance to avoid traffic, police interference, and toll booths. Kolanji started to drive on while others drowsed off. The deserted road ran straight for around 4 km, so the van gradually gained speed. Kolanji steered casually, looking at the road through the beam of the headlights. Kolanji felt tired and sleepy; he strained his eyes, but there was dullness. He closed his eyes for a second. THUD, BANG... The van missed the right turn, flew into the fields covered with *Semmai karuvai* plants, and came to a halt. No one knew what had happened. Everyone was crying in pain. The dust clouded the place.

The two guys who came behind them in a two-wheeler stopped the motorcycle and rushed to the spot to help them. They hesitated a little after seeing the ATM cash van and the armed guards. They checked the guards and driver, and they were unconscious. One of them said, "We should call the ambulance and the police." He took out his phone, and the other snatched it. "Wait, let us check the back of the vehicle. They are carrying money. We can take some and leave before others come." "No, it's dangerous; they will trace us. We should call the police." But the other one was not ready to listen to him. He went to the back of the vehicle and was surprised to see that there was no lock. They opened the latch and opened the door wide open. Since it was dark inside, both took out their cell phones and switched on the torch. Before they looked into the vehicle, they heard the screeching sound of the tyres, and a Tata Sumo came to a halt. People jumped down, shouting at them. The two-wheeler guys immediately switched off their torches, closed the door, and ran away.

The people surrounded the van and started to pull out Arul, Viji, Dhinesh, and Kolanji. Kolanji had a lot of damage, broken ribs, and a head injury, while others had violent injuries. None of them were wearing seat belts. The net over the windscreen protected them. One of them called the car, which was escorting the cash van in the front. They came rushing in five minutes. They all loaded the wounded and rushed off the place.

The rest of the party, around five in number, were instructed to stay back and guard the tiger and the vehicle. They relaxed for some time. Then they decided to check on the tiger. When they reached the door, they got the shock of their lives. The door was open. They looked at each other in shock. Their leader shone the torchlight, and they saw that the tiger was gone. They forgot about the package "The Tiger" in all the chaos. The tiger found its way out while all were attending to the wounded. The man shouted to his companions, "Hey, Tiger escaped." Terror gripped them. "Climb the trees. The tiger could be around here." They all ran hysterically and climbed the trees nearby. He then called someone over the phone and informed them of the situation. "They are instructing us to go in search of it." "Are they mad?" replied his companion. "I am not climbing down. We will sit out till dawn and inform them that we have searched the entire area, and the tiger was not found anywhere. I don't want to get killed by the tiger." Others affirmed him. So, they all sat to see the daybreak. After daybreak, they climbed the stretched-out branches of the tree and looked for the tiger. Then they called their boss and informed them that the tiger was not found anywhere. They climbed down the tree when the tow vehicle arrived. They cleared the van, and other evidence and hurriedly left the place.

THREE

Kidai madu is one of the main occupations in the Thirumanur union of Ariyalur District, Tamil Nadu. It is the herding of local species of cows and bulls. *Keethari*, the herdsman with a considerable number of cattle of his own, would also take the cattle from his village and nearby villages and go around throughout the year camping on the way in farmlands at the request of the farmers. The urine and cow dung become the manure for the fields. The owner of the land would pay for the cattle to stay on his land. If they cannot find such farmers, they camp in the open spaces, mostly near water sources.

The owners of the cattle who do not have land will hand over their cattle to *Keethari*. They do not have to pay much to the *Keethari*. The *Keethari* usually takes a *thadchanai* of a thousand and one rupees or five hundred and one rupees or one hundred and one on a plate with coconut, *Vetrilai pakku* (the betel leaves and betel nuts), and a couple of bananas to take the cattle into his herd.

The *Kari Naal* falls on the final day of the four-day harvest festival, Pongal, in Tamil Nadu. On this day, the Keethari, after offering prayers to their family deity, leads around 300 cattle, including those from nearby villages, on a year-long journey covering approximately 250 km.

Throughout the day, they graze the cattle in the green pastures and bring them back to the open fields or farmlands. Usually, they would camp in the agricultural fields for a couple of days when a farmer asked them to camp the cattle in their fields. When such stays are finished and the herd has to move, they move at night to avoid the traffic blockade the cattle would create.

Keethari always move with their utensils to prepare their food; a simple meal of boiled rice and *kulambu* will be enough for them. When they camp in the surroundings of their village, they will get food from their homes. They would also buy food from the local eateries. They sleep in the open at night. At night, to prevent the cattle from escaping or wandering, they bring two cows side by side and then tie the left front leg of one cow with the right front leg of the other. In some instances, when a cow or bull is arrogant, tying it with another cow or bull will hurt the other. So, they will tie the two front or hind legs to prevent them from running. The forest had no predators, so the herd casually moved around villages near Kolathur Forest because the forest in the Ariyalur district had no predators like tigers or leopards. The herd only encounters snakes, foxes, and wild boars. The cattle will deal with the foxes and the wild boar and need less help from the Keethari. However, they should be careful with the snakes. Some of them could be as big as the arms of a stout man. They always try to scare off the snakes. If they fail, they will use *suluki* to kill it. So, after finishing their dinner, the Keethari tied the legs of the cattle and slept peacefully.

Mani was a renowned Keethari, known for his honesty. He lived in Aravakurichi village. He had around sixty cattle of his own and also took the cattle of the villagers. His herd consisted mainly of half-grown calves, a few bulls, and cows—nearly 250 in number. They had been moving along the herd for the past three months, since January, after the Pongal festival. They have six more months before they hand over the cattle to their owners. This morning, they reached the village of Ullur.

Ullur is located ten kilometres to the west of Palikurichi. They had planned to stay the night and the next day and then move to the next village in the night. They chose to camp on the open land close to the Yeri. The land belonged to no one. The villagers used it for special occasions like *Theemithi* and other temple festivals. The open land was flattened and grassy. Thick bushes in the form of the *seemai karuvai* plants and saplings enclosed it on the rear and sides, and that would keep the cattle intact. Moreover, it was also on the road that went all the way to Thirumanur via Palikurichi, where they got their food and other supplies.

Mani stood 5' 7", dark, lean, strong, and determined. He knew all the places they camped from his childhood. His father and his uncle trained him from childhood. Mani and his elder brother Marthu used to join their father's Kidai on the weekends and school vacations. Their mother would drop them off by bus. They would cook chicken or mutton and pack the food for everyone. Then they would take the bus to the town, and from there they would take any available mode of transport—an auto, town bus, or minibus—to reach the camp. Sometimes, their father would wait at the bus stand to pick them up if their camp was close to the town or in the village where the bus could reach the least. On reaching the camp, they would spend the whole day there as a family.

In the late afternoon, after lunch, their mother boarded the bus that took her to the town, and from there, she took the last bus to their village. The boys would stay with their father and the herd till Sunday evening. Then, their father took them in the two-wheeler and dropped them off. He would stay for the night and leave for the camp in the morning, taking rice and kulambu for his friends. During vacations, the boys would stay till they got tired, for they never got tired until the holidays ended. They also had the company of the boys of the other Keethari. So naturally, they were attracted to this way of life.

After completing his schooling, Maruthu joined the Kidai of his father. After his father's death, Maruthu attended other men's Kidai, and Mani was still in his twelfth standard . After completing the twelfth standard, Mani was admitted to college, but he entered this business after discontinuing his studies in the first year. Now he was 46, and he was one of the few experienced Keethari in his locality. His team consisted of three men: Muthu, Rajesh, and Murali. Muthu and Rajesh were his childhood friends, who were well experienced in handling the cattle. However, Murali, on the other hand, was new to the field and had only been working for two years, so he had much to learn.

Just like any other night, Mani and his friends were preparing to camp that night in Ullur. Little did they know what awaited them that night. Except for Murali, others were familiar with this village. They had been camping exactly in the same place for years. Muthu and Murali checked the ropes, while Rajesh went around the cattle and bound them closer. Mani checked his mobile and said, "Murali, Go to Palikurichi and buy food and water. Get five idlis and an omelette for me and ask others what they want." Murali walked up to them and asked what they wanted for dinner. They asked for porotta, omelette, half-boil, and kalaki. Murali grabbed the 20-litre water can, hopped on his Super XL, and headed to Palikurichi village to purchase dinner. Mani said to Muthu and Rajesh, "I will stay with the cattle. You both go to the Yeri and refresh; after you return, I will go." Muthu replied, "We will keep the rope ready and then go." It took them almost ten minutes to pile up the rope, stretch it, and keep it ready to tie the legs of the cattle. After they had finished, they left for the Yeri, leaving Mani behind to watch the cattle.

Mani looked at his friends as they walked on the road towards the lake that was situated 500 metres away. The night was pitch-black around them. The torch provided by their phone illuminated their path. They walked slowly, listening to their favourite song on their phone. Muthu walked cheerfully, humming the song, and Rajesh sang the song to his full throat. They walked gaily and seemed to be enjoying the moment and the music.

Mani went around the cows armed with his stout stick and a rechargeable high-beam torch, which was charged and brought back in the evening. He found that a few cows had moved away from the herd and brought them together. He double-checked the cattle, throwing the torch light on them. Fully satisfied, he switched off the torch and squatted on the ground.

After a long, hot day, the night was colder and more pleasant. He looked around and waited for his friends to return. Then, he spread a tarpaulin sheet on the ground and collected the sticks, *suluki*, and *alakku kuchi* that his friends had left behind. He put them beside the tarpaulin and waited patiently.

The Keethari always carried a sturdy bamboo stick that was about his height. Besides that, they carried a *Suluki*, a long, sharp spear-like weapon with a barb at the tip, similar to the one in the fishing hook. It was usually used to kill snakes. The *alakku kuchi* is a long, straight bamboo with a sharp sickle tied to one end to cut down the twigs and leaves from the high branches of the trees. The *alakku kuchi* Mani had was 20 feet long. He kept them at a safe distance but within reach. He then took out the emergency light they used while cooking and eating and two full water bottles and deposited them on the tarpaulin. He opened one bottle and drank water. Then, he reached into his half trouser, which he wore as the inner, and put his hands in the pocket to bring out the beedi bundle and match. He pulled out one beedi, struck out a match, lit it, and lay down on the tarpaulin. He breathed in, took a lung full of smoke, and closed his eyes to feel the smoke inside. He lay there for around ten minutes, listening to the chirping of crickets. His peace was disturbed by the sound of the bells tied to the necks of the cattle. Something made them restless. He instantly stood up and casually walked towards the cattle, smoking the beedi. He thought that the cattle were disturbed by a snake or some other reptiles that were common in the area. He went, intending to comfort them, and to walk back. Suddenly, the cattle started to grow more nervous. They were frantically looking at the bushy side and starting to push back.

In that stampede, a few cattle stumbled and fell. It was then that Mani realised that the behaviour of his herd was new, and he was also reminded of the torch and the stick he had left behind. He threw the beedi, turned around, and doubled back to take them. On reaching the tarpaulin, he grabbed the torch in his left hand and the stick in his right. Then he changed his mind after seeing the *alakku kuchi* and *suluki*; he dropped the stick and grabbed them. As he turned around to check the situation in the torchlight, the cattle broke the line and started to run in all directions. Fortunately, they missed him in their run for life. Quickly, he switched on the torch, and the beam of light fell on the scene that he had never seen in all his life and maybe not even in the future. He saw a staggering young bull and a tiger almost clinging to the bull with its hind legs clawed on the back and its forelegs clasped around the neck. The tiger was biting the neck, bringing the bull to the ground at lightning speed SNAP. He could hear that sound in that silence. The neck of the bull broke, and it fell to the ground with a loud thud, with all four legs pointed to the sky. He could not believe what he saw. He had not heard of any tigers wandering in this locality. Though it is near Kolathur forest, it was free of predators, for the forest had no thick vegetation to feed deer and other animals, so there was no chance for the tigers or leopards to wander in the vicinity.

In all his life, he had not seen a tiger. However, he saw it in action that close, killing his cattle; he stood there dumbfounded. He felt like shouting Puli, Puli, or calling his friends, but he could not move a muscle. He stood there gazing at the happenings, his legs trembling and goosebumps all over his body, sweating from head to toe. Knowing his presence, the tiger threw a glance at him over its shoulder, lifted the bull, slung on his back, and started running towards the bushes. It was a stunning scene to watch the tiger lift the bull casually, twice the size of it. The tiger had hardly fifty feet to reach the bushes, and then it would vanish.

It was then that Mani came to his senses; he realised that the tiger had killed his cattle and challenged his skill as Keethari. As an experienced and established Keethari, he felt his ego crushed. He started chasing the tiger, calling his friends, "Rajesh, Muthu Puli da, come fast," in the highest pitch his throat could allow, and threw his suluki at the tiger. With his ego hurt and the fright given by the tiger, the aim was inaccurate, and the suluki missed the tiger and went between the legs of the tiger. The tiger tumbled and fell, with the bull's weight all over its body. The young bull's half-grown horns severed the tiger's left front shoulder. The tiger growled frantically, trying to release itself from the bull's horns. Mani sensed that the tiger was in trouble. Finally, after a little struggle, it tore off the skin and released itself from the horns. It growled in pain and started beating and clawing the dead bull madly.

Mani got more courage and dropped the torch to the ground to use both hands to hold the alakku kuchi. He ran towards the growling tiger, holding it in both hands firmly. When he reached the range to use his alakku kuchi, he stretched it in the direction of the tiger. The small but sharp sickle tied firmly on the other end touched the right hind legs of the tiger. Since the tiger was frantically busy releasing itself from the horns of the bull, it did not see Mani advancing towards it. He pulled it hard at the tiger. The sharp sickle made a deep cut. In pain, the tiger jumped and fell back, growling. It managed to spring back on its feet and attack the stick, which caused the pain, and then it realised that the attacker was the man and not the stick. It growled loudly at Mani, baring its teeth, and was about to charge at him. Mani understood that he was in danger, dropped the stick, turned around, and started to run, yelling in his full throat.

Meanwhile, his friends who went to freshen up were on their way back when they heard Mani and the growl of the tiger; they came running to the spot, shouting to help his friend. Murali was also riding back from Palikurichi. He saw the cattle running on the road. He was wondering what drove the cattle crazy. Hearing the shouts and seeing the tiger from a distance, he also rushed in, honking the horn of the two-wheeler. They all synchronised perfectly and entered the scene of action. Mani felt relieved to see his friend in the two-wheeler honking loudly, coming towards him at full speed, and his other friends running with their torches, shouting in full throat. Realising the sudden change of the scene and the presence of more men, the tiger left the place hurriedly, growling, abandoning its kill and its charge towards Mani. It disappeared into the thick bushes as mysteriously as it came in.

Mani fell to the ground, gasping for breath. His friends held him, and they all sat there for around ten minutes, holding Mani and comforting him. They kept their mobile phone torches on, scanning their surroundings fearfully. They could all hear the growling of the tiger. The sound faded gradually and eventually died. All four looked at each other. Murali asked, "Has the tiger gone?" Rajesh replied, "Who knows, maybe it may come back. It is not safe for us to be here. Muthu, get the water bottle." Murali looked around in fear. It was pitch-black everywhere; the darkness they were used to now posed a danger.

Muthu grabbed the water bottle, opened it, and sprinkled a handful of water on Mani's face. Murali had dropped the two-wheeler. The food parcels he brought fell, and the water can was hurdled under the two-wheeler, but it was safe and undamaged. Rajesh ran fast and fetched the torch. Mani shouted at him, "Rajesh, are you mad? Tiger could be here watching us." Rajesh replied, "We need the torch to check the surroundings. Mobile torch will not reach". Murali said, "We should get our suluki and alakku kuchi. That is all we have in defence." "No, leave it," replied Mani. "We cannot go that far. The tiger may attack again; we will wait here till dawn." Rajesh asked, "What if we sit here and the tiger attacks us? We will not have anything to defend us. We should also get the two-wheeler, the food, and the water can."

Mani said, "Then I will fetch them." His friends did not accept the idea. Murali said, "You look exhausted. If the tiger comes, you will not be able to run. Let me go." Everyone except Mani accepted it. "I am the only one who knows where they are," he said, sounding correct. Further, he said, "One of you can join me, Murali and Rajesh; you stay here. Be careful. Do not watch us; we will manage. Look at your surroundings. Muthu and I will grab things."

Everyone accepted the idea. Mani grabbed his sturdy bamboo stick and handed down the sticks of Murali and Rajesh to them. Muthu grabbed his stick in his right hand and the torch in his left. Muthu switched on the torch, and Mani nodded. "Stay behind me." Both sprinted to the spot near the bull's carcass. Mani looked for the suluki and alakku kuchi, while Muthu looked at the surroundings with fear. He could feel his heart thudding. Mani saw the suluki under the bull and pulled it out. He pointed to the alakku kuchi and said, "Muthu, grab it." Then both ran back to the men, waiting.

On the way, they stopped near the two-wheeler, and Mani handed the stick and suluki to Muthu. Muthu scanned the surroundings with the torch, while Mani picked up the bag containing food parcels and kept it on the ground. He then hurriedly moved the water can, lifted the two-wheeler, and loaded the water can in the gap between the seat and steering, which was provided for that purpose. Meanwhile, Muthu grabbed the bag and hung it on the side hook. Mani started pushing the two-wheeler, and Muthu followed him. Both reached out to their friends. Murali said, "You could have started the two-wheeler and rode here." Mani replied, "Fool, if I start the motorcycle, the tiger will hear it." Murali sheepishly said, "I forgot it." Mani thoughtfully said, "We cannot stay here." He grabbed the mobile from Murali and checked the time; it said 9.46 p.m. "We should find a place to hide till morning." Murali asked, "Can't we go to the village?" Mani replied thoughtfully, "No, the tiger might be around anywhere. It is not safe going in that direction." Mani started to think of the surroundings and the nearest building available. Muthu interrupted his thoughts: "Mani, the temple... on the way to the Yeri, it will be big enough to accommodate us all. On the way here, I saw the gates were not locked, and they were only latched." Mani thought for a while, "Yes, I almost forgot it. Come on, grab the things; we will make a run to that temple. Muthu, take some ropes to tie the gates."

Everyone grabbed the sticks; Murali got the food, and Muthu got the water bottles. They all ran, reached the main road, turned to the left, ran for about a hundred feet, and reached the temple. Murali and Muthu led, while Mani and Rajesh took the rear. Muthu opened the latch of the gate of the temple, and all four hurdled inside. As they entered, the bats residing there flew off. The place smelled of the droppings of the bats. The temple was a little small. It had a *sannathi* that was locked with a wooden door, and in the front, there was a small hall with a low ceiling that could fit up to eight people. The walls on either side had sixteen small, triangle-shaped openings arranged in two rows of eight to serve as ventilation. The alakku kuchi could not be kept inside, so they left it on the steps. After closing the gates and tying them with the rope, Mani pulled the bottom side of the alakku kuchi through the gate, leaving the sickle outside.

Mani looked around for any other openings and was glad to see that the place was safe. Everyone relaxed and switched off the torches, except the emergency light. They all sat on the floor, avoiding the gate. Mani asked, "What now?" Rajesh replied, "Call the police, the president of Palikurichi Village panchayat, and our friends in Ullur." Mani switched off the torch on his mobile. "You all take food. I will make the phone calls and join you." Mani was busy making calls. Muthu told Murali and Rajesh to eat and waited until Mani finished his calls.

When Murali and Rajesh almost finished eating, Mani had finished making calls. Mani said, "The police did not trust my words. However, they promised to come early in the morning. Same answer from the friends in the village." Muthu intervened, "Have you told them you had wounded it?" Mani nodded negatively. "I have already lost my bull, and I really do not want to end up in jail." Further, he thoughtfully said, "Where did the tiger come from, and how did it get here? With no animals to hunt, what will it do?" Rajesh said, "That is why it got our cattle." Mani told them, "Now take some rest. We have a lot of work to do in the morning." Murali and Rajesh finished their food and washed their hands. Mani and Muthu took their share of food and started eating thoughtfully.

The following day, at the first light, Mani and his friends walked out to the spot. They were relieved to see that the cattle had reached the camp. They went straight to the carcass of the bull and were shocked to see that half of it had been eaten. Mani started to check the cattle. The villagers started pouring in and gathered around. Mani and his friends started explaining the happenings. At around 8 a.m., the police arrived at the spot and started investigating. After being thoroughly convinced that the kill was made by an animal, they informed the forest department.

The officials from the forest department were shocked to see the scene. They took pictures of the pug marks and then found the blood trail left by the wounded tiger and followed it. By seeing the blood in the horns of the bull, they concluded that the tiger was wounded by the bull. Nevertheless, they could not locate the tiger. In the following month, trap cameras were installed in the nearby villages of Ullur, but the tiger remained untraceable. They had no other option but to wait until a similar incident happened. However, nothing happened in the following days. Eventually, the issue was conveniently forgotten.

FOUR

It was a Monday morning in the Tamil month of Panguni, the last week of March. Karthi, a thirteen-year-old boy, lived in the village of Karuppukudi near the Keelakolathur forest. He was studying eighth standard at the middle school in the same village. Like every day, he woke up at 5:00 in the morning. He had an urge to pee, though he felt lazy; the pressure in his abdomen compelled him to rise from his bed.

He walked to the back door, unlocked it, and made his way to the far end of the backyard, close to the neem tree, avoiding the toilet. While standing there, he relieved himself, rubbing his sleepy eyes with one hand and then running it through his hair. As he looked around, his eyes met with a large animal sitting under the shade of the trees, about thirty feet away. At first, he thought it was a dog, but then he realised it was too big to be a dog. Suddenly, the branches of the tree moved, and the moonlight illuminated the animal, revealing it to be a tiger staring right at him. He was terrified to see a tiger so close.

Karthi's drowsiness disappeared, and he swiftly turned around and ran towards the back door of the house, hurriedly entering and locking it behind him. He breathed heavily out of fear. He could feel his heart pounding in his chest as he breathed heavily out of fear. The tiger banged on the door repeatedly as it was trying to break in. Karthi stood there transfixed, watching the door shake violently under the weight of the tiger. Then there was a heavy bang, and the next minute, the door broke.

Karthi fell to the floor, and the door landed on him. With one spring, the tiger stood at the door. Karthi lay under the door, crushed under the weight of the tiger and the door. He cried, "Amma, save me." He cried loudly and continuously. His mother opened the front door and rushed in, followed by his sister, Ilakiyaa. "Karthi, wake up.... What happened?" His mother shook him violently. "Tiger killed me, Amma," cried Karthi. Amma and Ilakiyaa laughed at him. "You were dreaming. There are no tigers in our district or in the surrounding districts. Come on, get up. You will be late. You should give the milk to the society milkman on time." Ilakiyaa remarked, "People often believe that dreams had in the early morning come true. Is this true, Amma? If so, will Karthi's dream also come true?" Karthi started crying. The mother planted a *kottu* on Ilakiyaa's head, went near Karthi, and caressed his hair. "There is no tiger." "No, Amma, my English sir, told about tigers and how they killed men in the villages while teaching a lesson on Jim Corbett." "Those were the old days when tigers roamed free, but now no tigers are around. Get up and start your work for the day. I must prepare your food and then go to work. Karthi, Appa is going to Ariyalur, so you need not attend school today. You take the cows and goats for grazing. "No, Amma, today is Akka's turn. I am going to school today." "Akka has a public exam on Monday. She must go to school. Today, you take the cattle," said the mother. "Please, da, just one day. I will take care of the cattle after exams," pleaded Ilakiyaa. Karthi was adamant, and nothing could persuade him to take the cattle.

Mostly like Karthi, the children of Karuppukudi were busy getting ready for their routine chores in the early hours. On school days, they would escape to school after their breakfast. But on holidays, they had plenty of work to do. They usually get up at 4 a.m. to milk the cows, clean the cowshed, and then take the milk to the society milkman. Then, they would fetch water from the panchayat taps provided on the street and fill all the available pots and pans in the house. Then, they sat down to wash the vessels used the previous night for cooking dinner. After preparing the breakfast, their parents would head out to work in the fields or as labourers on the construction sites in town. After breakfast, the children would take their goats and cows to graze, and no gender bias was evident in this daily routine.

Most of the work at home was done by the children. Throughout the day, they grazed the cattle, carrying their lunch in their boxes and the water bottles covered with a piece of jute sack soaked in water to keep the water cool.

In the late afternoon, they took the cattle home to be milked. By the time the parents returned from the fields, the children had already carried water from the street tap, filled the vessels, and cleaned the utensils used in the morning to cook breakfast. After finishing these works, they sat down to study. This was the case for the children whose parents worked in the fields. The children, whose parents work in town, do all this work alone. They even prepare dinner and wait for the arrival of their parents. Their parents usually come by the last bus, dead tired from their day's work.

The children in the town love the holidays, but it's quite the opposite for these children. They prefer going to school, where they can take a break from their daily chores, learn new things, and play with their friends. They finish their work in the morning, take the cattle to the grazing lands, tie them with a liberal rope, and then head to school. During the break, they check on the cattle and return to the school.. Unlike the town kids, the village kids love to stay in school, for them, school is the only place where they can enjoy their time. In contrast to the town kids, who find weekends and holidays exciting, these children don't like weekends because they have to work on the farm and graze the cattle in the scorching sun, and it would be worse during summer vacations.

Ilakiyaa, Karthi's sister, studied twelfth standard in the higher secondary school in Kovilur. Her village had only a middle school, so like all her village kids, after completing the eighth standard, she got admitted to the school in Kovilur. Every day, she and her friends had to walk four kilometres to reach the school. Although they had a free pass, the only town bus that plied that route couldn't be taken because the bus would take them to Kovilur at 9.50 a.m., while the school started at 9.30 a.m. Hence, they were forced to walk those four kilometres. In the evening, there was no bus available, so they walked back another four kilometres. Only a few of them could afford bicycles. All of them were waiting for the free cycles issued by the government. Despite this, Ilakiyaa was determined to attend school and didn't want to miss any classes. She was one of the top scorers in her class and had already written her twelfth standard board exam with just one paper left, which was scheduled for the following Monday. However, today, Ilakiyaa's mother asked her to graze the cattle.

The teachers knew the situation of the students, so they asked them to come to school for revision, but it was actually to keep the girls from doing chores. However, today, she had no other options. Her brother was not helping her, so she took the textbooks with her to graze the cattle near the forest. The land near the forest was an ideal grazing spot since there would be no disturbance, and the cattle didn't require her attention. She usually grazed the cattle there when she had too much homework to do. No fields were nearby, so she need not be worried about the cattle. She would study her lessons while the cattle wandered near the forest and grazed.

Ilakiyaa took her alakku kuchi and other belongings and led her cattle to the outskirts of Karuppukudi village. She walked with her seven cows and twelve goats along the main road for about fifteen minutes, then turned onto the mud road and arrived at her favourite spot after another ten-minute walk.

The land that she was about to graze her cattle was open, with trees such as palmyra, karuvelam, pungai, and neem scattered and providing adequate shade and shelter for the cattle. The land was mostly covered with shrubs, lantana bushes, avaram plants, and seemai karuvai, along with grasses all over the place; it made a perfect place for grazing the cattle. But the villagers avoided grazing their cattle there because of the distance, as it was roughly three kilometres from Karuppukudi.

Palmyra trees were commonly found in the region and would often grow in rows. These trees were highly valuable, as all their parts were useful and had a variety of uses. For instance, their leaves were used to create items such as fans, boxes, and mats. Panam *kilangu* was also edible and had medicinal value. During the summer season, people would harvest it for *nongu* and *pathaneer*. The leaf stalks of the tree were used to create fences, but they had razor-sharp edges that could easily cut a person to the bone. Therefore, only trained men could climb these trees to bring down *nongu* and *pathaneer*. Once, an enthusiastic boy climbed to bring down *nongu*. While climbing down, his foot came into contact with the leaf stack and ended up with sixteen stitches. Such trees were lined up near the bridge and also near the mud road. Ilakiyaa found that the trees were cleaned and harvested for *nongu*. The leaf stalks were scattered carelessly.

The mud road Ilakiyaa took was recently laid at the far end of the land, near the Kolathur forest. This road went to the Kasan Kadu, the limestone mines, and further to the forest. On this road, near a pungai tree, was a small bridge to allow the stream to flow through during rainy days. This bridge was her study area. The pungai tree gave her an excellent, cosy cover from the hot sun. There, she settled her books, lunch box, and water bottle. She went to the cows that had already started to graze, held the neck rope of the cattle, and tied it to one of their front legs to prevent them from running away. After she tied up all the cows and goats, she went to the bridge and started her studies. She need not worry about the cattle for the next few hours. When it was past 12, she decided to cut down a few twigs of the neem tree for goats. She grabbed her alakku kuchi, stood up, walked to the neem tree, and cut down the neem twigs and the seemai karuvai fruits. The goats ate them happily, and she walked back to her place.

The cows started grazing in the area far from her, and one of them went near the mud road and started grazing. Ilakiyaa saw that the cow was moving towards the recently cleaned palmyra trees. The leaves and the leaf stalks were scattered around in all sizes. She was worried that the cow might wound itself, so she stood up and walked towards it to clean it. She went near and started to pick up the stalks. Then she heard the low grunt of an animal from behind. She turned around and saw the enormous face of a tiger crouching on the mud road. For a second, she thought she was dreaming. But a loud growl from the tiger told her it was real. Since she was standing behind the two trunks of the palmyra tree, the tiger could not see her. The next few seconds went fast, and the tiger, with a few slow steps, suddenly charged towards the cow.

Without knowing the consequences, Ilakiyaa ran towards the tiger impulsively and struck it with the leaf stalk she had in her hand. The tiger was stunned by her move. The razor-sharp leaf stalk struck the face, and the tiger growled with pain and anger. Its face has now turned red from its blood and anger. It growled at her angrily. She dropped the leaf stalk and ran under the small bridge to hide. She knew it was not safe.

She saw a pungai tree a hundred feet away and ran towards it. The tiger saw her running. It abandoned the attack on the cow and, with one leap, followed her. Ilakiyaa saw the tiger behind her and increased her speed to reach the tree. Though she reached the tree, it was not easy to climb. The tiger grabbed her back, and she fell down. It bit her face, and its front paw clawed through her chest with hatred. She lay still there, blood oozing from the deep cuts, struggling to breathe. The tiger left her, walked towards the cattle, and stood looking at them. It had lost interest in the cattle and walked towards the bushes far behind the pungai tree where Ilakiyaa was lying. It rubbed its head in the leaves with pain and sat there for some time. Ilakiyaa was still choking, moaning, and wailing in pain. The tiger stood up, walked to Ilakiyaa, and killed her. It sat by her side and started licking the blood off her body and the blood that gushed through her deep wounds. Then, on a sudden impulse, the tiger picked up the girl and dashed off.

The cattle could not find Ilakiyaa in the evening and slowly walked home without her. Karthi was shocked. He ran to the spot, only to find her things that were deposited on the bridge. He dashed back to the village and called the family members for help. The parents were informed over the phone. The family members rushed to the spot with Karthi and found that the girl was not in the vicinity; they saw her books and untouched lunch. Since the presence of the tiger was not known, the first thought that came to the minds of the villagers was elopement and abduction. The villagers started to tell stories about her talking with boys, which mercilessly destroyed her character. However, her parents still filed a complaint at the Thirumanur police station, and a missing case was registered. A week rolled by, but her whereabouts were not known. Gradually, her parents started to believe that she must have eloped with someone and that she was happily living somewhere.

FIVE

The Panchayat school is situated on the outskirts to the north of Karuppukudi. The school stood on the main road, half a kilometre away from the village. It was a middle school with two small, old buildings. The buildings were lined up parallel to the road, leaving around a 200-foot gap between the road and the buildings. It was used as the playground for the schoolchildren. One of the buildings that stood closer to the gate had two classrooms, and the other far inside had three classrooms. The school also had two kitchens for preparing noon meals. The kitchen opposite the three-classroom building was new, and the other near the gate was old and abandoned.

Beside the three-classroom building, there were toilets for girls. Behind these toilets was the *odai*, which takes excess water from Madiyeri to Ulliyeri in Melaiyur, the next village. This *odai* is dry and thickly inhabited by seemai karuvai plants. Parallel to this, *odai* ran the road to Melaiyur, which was four kilometres away.

On Friday morning, the children started coming in; they deposited their bags on the verandah and started playing. The sweeper women had started cleaning the classrooms. Jeeva, studying in the eighth standard, saw the old man sleeping on the verandah of the new kitchen building. He went to him and woke him up. "Thatha, it's time; get up." The old man opened his eyes; there was no spirit in them. He had a bushy beard and long hair. His eyes were evident of his starvation. He slowly got up and folded his two blankets, one to spread out on the floor and another to cover himself. He kept them in the corner of the verandah and strolled out of the school towards the tamarind tree that stood opposite the school. Then, the school's everyday activities started while the old man waited, lying under the tamarind tree.

The old man was Alagar, from Melaiyur. He was abandoned by his family and friends. Some would say he deserves it. Some pity him. Even his old associates avoided him. He was once a notorious dacoit. The villagers were only suspicious of his activities. Until one day, he was caught red-handed, and his family threw him out.

Alagar was the youngest son of his family. After his father's death, he got Kasan Kadu, the three acres of land, as his share. He was happily married to Vembu and had a boy, Ajith, and two daughters, Chitra and Renu. He planted cotton and sugarcane and worked as labour on construction sites. Everything went well until his elder daughter eloped and married a boy from another community. The village got divided and started vandalising each other's homes. The police made a lot of arrests, and cases were filed. All the while, the couple was on their honeymoon.

Alagar was taken to drinking, and all his earnings went to drinking. He drank throughout the day and started quarrelling with his wife. He would find every reason to pick a quarrel. He would throw anything that came in handy at her. The children were not spared, and the boy was the ultimate victim. When the time for Renu's marriage came up, he sold half of Kasan Kadu to Velmurugan. Then, in a couple of years, he sold the rest of the land to the same man to pay for the cost of sending Ajith to Dubai as a labourer.

Velmurugan employed Alagar to take care of the land. They fenced the three acres and planted coconut, teak, mango, guava, and other trees. They also built a small house using cement sheets. Then, Velmurugan planned to move in with his family. They started to construct a big house. Alagar helped Velmurugan coordinate and supervise the work. Soon, Alagar developed the habit of taking excess money from Velmurugan, which strained their relationship, and he moved out to work on other construction sites. His son started sending money to the family. He spent all the money on drinking. He always had a band of friends and started spending all the money on them. This news reached his son, and he stopped sending money. Everyone thought he would calm down, but he continued his way of living. His new friends had a notorious background, so everyone guessed how they earned money.

Then, the coronavirus started to spread, and the government announced a lockdown. Alagar and his gang lost their jobs and could not carry out their illegal activities. On that occasion, they planned to break into Velmurugan's house. Since it was a lonely house and Alagar was familiar with it and the people, they were sure of success. Even if the family woke up and called someone in Karuppukudi or the police for help, it would take at least half an hour to reach the house. By this time, they could finish off everything and escape.

Previously, Alagar visited the house to check the number of inmates under the pretext of asking for a loan from Velmurugan. Velmurugan refused to give him money and advised him. Alagar was happy that the whole family stayed there to spend the lockdown. Their only problem was Maruthu, so they had to wait till Maruthu left the family alone.

After a week's wait, Alagar observed that Maruthu had left for Aravakurichi to stay with his brother. The gang prepared to execute their plan that night. Around 1:00 a.m., they reached the house. The house stood alone, with no dogs or Maruthu to guard. They jumped over the compound and reached the gate. They tore off the metal mosquito net on the gate, put their hands through the grill, and reached for the padlock. They tried to break it using an iron rod but failed, and then they used a hacksaw blade to cut the lock. After fifteen minutes of hard work, the lock was broken. Then they entered and reached the front door. The door before them was a conventional teak double door. They used the chisel to break the latches on the door below. Then they inserted a sledge and slowly forced it through the door. Finally, the door gave up, and slowly, they moved in. The hall was empty; the four bedrooms, two on the ground floor and two on the first floor, were also closed. First, they all checked the two bedrooms on the ground floor and found them empty. And then they climbed the stairs and reached the two rooms on the first floor. Those rooms were also empty. They checked the bathrooms and kitchens. Then they came to the back door that leads to the terrace. They were surprised to see that the doors were locked from the outside. They looked at each other, and they realised that they were trapped. They ran out to check the gate; it was locked from the outside.

Soon, people gathered from the village, and then the police came and arrested the robbers. Velmurugan and the villagers were shocked to see Alagar and his friends. Then Alagar got bail and came out of prison. The family and friends avoided him. His son strictly told his mother to throw him out of the house. He had nowhere to go. And thus, he ended up taking refuge in this school building. Only a few gave him food or money; one of his close relatives or his old friends would give him food, but not daily, so mostly he starved. But he never asked or begged for money or food. He never went to his house again. He, too, felt that he deserved it.

He always spent the night in the lonely school building. In the morning, he would go out before the students came in and then return in the evening after school. Everyone, including the headmaster and village people, told him to stay away from school, but he never listened. One day, the noon meal was in excess. Jeeva asked the headmaster of the school, "Sir, can we give excess food to Thatha instead of throwing it? He doesn't have anyone to give food to or money to buy food.". The headmaster thought, "I was also thinking about it. Find a plate for him." Jeeva took a plate, went to the tap and washed it, went to the cook, and filled the plate. He called his friend, "Nathan, run to the tamarind tree. Thatha will be lying there. Bring him in. Tell him the HM sir called him."

The old man walked slowly, with no life in his eyes. When the children gave him the plate, he could hardly hold it. He broke into tears. "It's been three days since I ate anything." He started eating slowly. The children went to the headmaster and told him the old man's words. The HM said, "Whenever there is excess food, give him a plate. You need not ask my permission. But remember only when the food is left out." From that day on, he was given food on a plate only when there was excess. And it was almost every day, except for Fridays. On Fridays, the children were served rice and sambar, and since they found it tasty, no food would be left over for him. Consequently, he had to go without food on Fridays, Saturdays, and Sundays. Sometimes, the students who felt pity for him would bring him leftover food from their homes.

Since it was Friday afternoon, there was no excess food. The schoolchildren fondly eat the rice and sambar. But that day, he felt very hungry; he laid down, anticipating a call from a child, 'Thatha, come and have some food'. But that didn't happen that day. He waited until the class started. Then he got up, walked slowly to the nearby field, drank some water from the pump, and sat there in the shade of the tree till the evening.

In the evening, he walked slowly back to school. Instead of going around and entering through the gate, he got down the odai, walked through the seemai karuvai plants, entered the back side of the school, and came to the kitchen building. He took the blankets, spread them on the floor, and laid on them.

On Saturday, a relative took pity on him and bought him a packet of biscuits. Sunday went as usual without any food. That evening, he felt very exhausted. He spread his blanket and laid on it. He didn't know whether he slept or lay unconscious on the verandah of the kitchen. Somewhere in the middle of the night, he woke up. Or perhaps something woke him—hunger or a sense of danger—he didn't know. But he is too weak to stand up. So he laid still, looking at the ceiling, trying to see through the darkness. What danger could come? He had been sleeping in that place for more than a year. Moreover, he thought he had nothing to lose except life.

He turned his eyes, traced the edges of the ceiling, and then moved to the branches of the neem tree next to him. He was too weak to move his hands and legs. He slowly turned his head to look at the playground. Dim moonlight made the surroundings appear in dark traces. His eyes caught on a dark object lying on the ground in the shade of the neem tree. It was moving or creeping slowly. The object had a long tail that moved from left to right in the air. It growled when his eyes landed on it. Slowly, it sat up on its haunches. He realised it was a tiger. He wanted to jump to his feet, push the tiger down, and claim the neem tree. But after all his effort, all he could do was sit up. The next instant, he felt the tiger land on him. The weight of the tiger crushed him. Then its flanks were buried in his throat, he gasped for breath, and its claws were buried on his shoulder. His mind wanted to kick the tiger and release him from the grip; SNAP, the spinal cord broke, and the old man was out of his misery. Without changing its grip, the tiger lifted him, slung over his back, and walked slowly without a rush. It entered the odai through the seemai karuvai plants. The man's vesti got stuck in the thorns, and the tiger tore off, crossed the road, and ran towards the forest area.

The following day, children came to school after the weekend. While the children started playing, Jeeva and his friend Abhishek saw the blankets spread on the kitchen verandah. "Jeeva, Thatha forgot to fold it," said Abhishek. "You fold it and keep it aside." Abhishek folded the blankets and kept them aside. The headmaster and other teachers came in, the school started, and the old man did not turn up for lunch in the afternoon. The students did not see him in the evening. The next day, they almost forgot about him.

SIX

Ariyalur district is rich in sedimentary and gypsum rocks. Approximately 15 million years ago, this land was under the sea; then, the seawater receded, and the sea animals and the animals that lived on land died and later became fossils. Thus, the Ariyalur district became a paleozoological garden. Many fossilised plants, animals, and dinosaur eggs were unearthed here.

The rich gypsum in this area has attracted several cement companies. The district has seven cement companies, including the one run by the Government of Tamil Nadu. Each of these companies has two units of factories to produce cement.

These companies offered competitive prices to the farmers to buy their lands to mine gypsum. These farmers always relied on the monsoonal rains to grow their dry crops. So, they readily sold their lands to these companies and settled in their lives.

Apart from these seven companies, a few companies near Trichy bought lands in these areas, mined the gypsum, and transported it to their factories through tipper trucks.

The Ven cement works, located near Samayapuram on the Trichy-Chennai national highways, had a mine in the lands bought from farmers of the villages of Karuppukudi, Mettukadu, and Narasingapuram. They mined these lands for three years and transported the gypsum to their factories. Then, they bought land near Kalakkudi. These lands were very close to their factories. So, they stopped mining in Karuppukudi and transferred the staff to Kalakkudi. They just employed a couple of security guards and closed the mines.

Muthu and Karuppaiyan were the security guards employed at the mines. They had a schedule of working three days each, taking turns, and sharing the remaining day on alternate weeks. They had a dog that kept them company. It was a puppy when they first saw it. Some of the villagers must have abandoned it on the outskirts of the village. One day, it just came to them out of nowhere. They started feeding it with the left out food, and later, they counted it as a member and shared the food with the dog. It had grown to its prime in two years. It helped by alerting them when the local boys sneaked in for a bath.

Visitors were rare, and they faced no significant issues while guarding the area. So, everything went peacefully. However, they had to be cautious during weekends and school holidays, as the boys from nearby villages would sneak in to play and swim in the lake. The mine consisted of a few structures, including a shed for the watchman, living quarters, an office building, and a garage. These buildings stood a hundred metres away from the watchman shed. The mining area was situated five hundred metres away from the buildings.

Karuppaiyan finished his shift on Sunday, and Muthu had to take over on Monday at 8 a.m. Monday morning, at around 7:30, Muthu started from his home to relieve him. He packed his things for a four-day stay. His wife packed his meals for the first two days. He had his breakfast and packed his lunch and dinner. His wife prepared rice and *kulambu* for the first day, which he would eat for lunch, and the leftovers would be eaten for dinner. For the second day, she prepared *pulli soru*, boiled rice mixed with tamarind paste, a traditional food that was usually prepared, packed, and taken while travelling; this rice would last a couple of days. He had to cook his meals for the other two days, so he packed the groceries and vegetables.

After double-checking his bags, he picked them up and started looking for his two-wheeler keys. To his surprise, he couldn't find them in their usual spot. He thought it might be the doing of his children, who might have thrown them somewhere. He began searching for them, and his wife joined in the search, but they could not locate them. He started to get wild with his children. He then looked at his watch and realised it was getting late. So, he gave up the search, called his friend, and requested that he drop him off at the mines.

When Muthu arrived at the mines, he found Karuppaiyan waiting impatiently. The dog came running to him, started licking his feet, and went around him. Muthu patted and stroked the dog. Karuppaiyan said, "Why are you late? What happened to your two-wheeler?" He pointed to the dog and said, "You know he found a pair." Muthu replied, "Wait. First, let me finish the attendance formalities. Then we can talk."

He hurriedly walked to the BAS, pressed his finger on the scanner, and marked his attendance. He was late by forty minutes. "The children threw the two-wheeler key somewhere. We searched for it, and then I asked my friend to drop me off." "How will you manage without a two-wheeler? Shall I leave my two-wheeler with you? Your friend can drop me off," asked Karuppaiyan. Muthu replied, "Don't worry. It's just four days. I can manage. I bought everything I needed on the way. So, no problem."

Muthu thanked his friend and told him to go home. Karuppaiyan left for his home after finishing the formalities. Muthu unpacked his things, put on his uniform, and then walked around the buildings to check them, and the dog happily followed him. Then he went along the fence to find the damage caused by the local men and boys to sneak in and take a bath in the mine's lake.

Every time they mend the fence, the locals damage it again to sneak in. Muthu and Karuppaiyan had repeatedly asked the officials to install cameras in selected places along the fence and near the lake. But the management turned a deaf ear to them. They knew that if someone drowned in the lake, they would be held responsible for it and penalised. The lake in the deep mines was unsafe and not a natural lake. While mining, the miners would get a lot of springs, and these water-filled, low-lying areas of the mines eventually resulted in the formation of the lake. So, there are rocks and gaps underneath the water surface. The water was dark green due to algae and slippery. When someone walks over it, they may slip off, or their legs would get stuck, and they could be pulled in and easily drowned.

Muthu and Karuppaiyan were always worried that the management and the locals were unaware of the potential danger and did not listen to their warnings. Muthu went around the fence, reached his shed, brought a chair, and sat under the tree near the gate. From there, he could easily see if someone had sneaked in. The dog went around sniffing and came back to lay by his side. For the rest of the day, there was not much activity for Muthu. The dog went outside and, after a long absence, came back with its pair. The bitch it brought was also stray, brown, and skinny. They both played around.

In the evening, Muthu prepared black tea since there was no milk, ate some snacks he had brought, and threw biscuits to the dogs. At seven, he knew his food was only enough for him, and there were two mouths to be fed. So, he boiled some rice, scrambled an egg, mixed it in the boiled rice, and gave it to the dogs. Both dogs ate to their full. He finished his dinner and again sat outside his shed. The TV inside the shed was positioned in such a way that he could watch it from the gate. So, he started killing time watching the series. The dogs slept by his side. At eleven, Muthu went inside the shed, locked the door, removed his shirt, and lay comfortably on the bed while the dogs slept peacefully on the steps of the shed. Muthu lay on the bed, listening to the chirping of the crickets and the multi-tone croaks of the frogs. He got used to it; it was a lullaby to him. He slept peacefully.

In the middle of the night, he woke up to a sound similar to that of a dog being hit by something. He lay on the bed and started to listen, and everything was silent. He thought it was his dream, or the dogs must be playing, and then he felt the urge of nature's call. There were no toilets attached to the shed. He was supposed to use the one in the living quarters. But at night, he always preferred to stay in the open. He opened the door of his shed and was surprised that the dogs were not there. He thought that they must have sneaked out. He then walked to the opposite side and urinated. He sat on the chair that he left near the gate. Then he took his torch and went around the living quarters and the garage. There was nothing to be robbed; no such attempts were made, but it was his routine.

Muthu went to bed again, but he didn't get sleep. Only then did he realise the unusual silence of the night, missing the familiar chirping of crickets. He tossed and turned in bed, unable to fall asleep, and the time seemed to drag on. Suddenly, he heard the faint sound of stones being displaced and tumbling down in the mine beneath. It sounded like some animal was climbing down the mine area. He closed his eyes and strained his ears. After a few minutes, the sound seized, and it was silence. He then heard the sound of an animal drinking water from the lake. He thought it must be the dogs. They must be going around, for there was no chance of other animals at this odd hour. He laid still and followed the sound. The sound lasted a few minutes, then silence, and it resumed and then seized again after a few minutes. Then, he could hear the stones again and assumed that the dogs were on the move. They were probably climbing up. Then it was perfect silence. Time passed, and gradually, he dozed off.

Again, his sleep was disturbed by some sound. This time, he heard the sound of metal falling onto the floor. He guessed that the sound came from the garage. Only there were a few old metal parts of the trucks. He knew that the window in that room was open. It must be the dogs. But he wondered how they could get in there.

The garage was previously the office, with a 2-tonne window AC attached to the window. When they shifted the office to the new building, they dismantled the AC and fixed a door in the gap, and now the hinges of the door were broken, and it was left open. They must have sneaked in through that opening. But that window was too high for them to jump in. With thoughts running through his mind, he sat on his cot.

Suddenly, another thought flashed in Muthu's mind: what if it was burglars? They knew he was alone. His mind took a double standard; it wanted to check the cause of the sound, but it also warned him that it would be dangerous to go out and check. He was confused a bit. Anyway, he decided to check the room. He gathered his courage, grabbed the torch and keys, opened the door, stepped out of the shed, and walked towards the living quarters. He went straight to the garage and stood near the door. There was no sound from inside, and he was not sure if he could open the door and check. Then, after some hesitation, he put his ears to the door to listen to the sounds. But it was silent inside. To be on the safe side, he decided to check the room through the open window. He switched on his torchlight and looked through the window, but there was nothing unusual.

Muthu stood there, confused, wondering if it was his dream. He checked his surroundings with his torchlight. He felt everything was fine, except the dogs were missing. He then walked to the mine, threw the light down at the lake, and scanned the areas his torchlight could reach; still, the dogs were nowhere to be seen. It was then that he heard a dull thud. He turned around, flashed his light, checked the window, and walked slowly towards it, slowly past the water tank. Then he saw something moving in the far-off bushes near the garage building. He stood still and shined his torch at the bush. He expected to see the dogs. But there, he saw a single bright eye of an animal staring at him from the shade of the bushes. It was crouching motionless, with only its tail moving. He could not guess the animal from its shadowy form. By now, the animal had slowly started to move.

Muthu stood still and stared at it. It was not a dog, he thought; it was something new that he had never seen before. And then the animal moved, and a tiger's face was now visible in the torchlight beam. He felt heat engulfing his body and started to sweat. He could not believe his eyes. "Am I dreaming?' he asked himself. The loud growl cleared his doubts about the tiger and brought him to his senses. The tiger started its charge towards him. He realised the happenings, looked around, ran back towards the overhead water tank, and climbed the ladder. The tiger followed him. With one leap, the tiger's front claws touched his foot. Muthu managed to reach the top of the tank and looked down at the tiger. It was trying to climb the ladder, growling at him furiously. He thanked God that he made it to the tank on time. But the tiger was still growling at him, standing on its hind legs on the ground and the front legs on the ladder. The sight of it frightened him; he looked around to grab something to throw at it. He could see only the heavy concrete slab that covered the maintenance hole of the tank. He lifted it with difficulty, moved it towards the ladder, and slid it along the metal ladder. The slab hit the tiger in the front legs, toppled, again hit the tiger's head, and fell to the ground with a loud thud. The tiger was stunned by the attack and ran towards the fence.

Muthu lay down, his body covered in sweat and his heart racing loudly in his ears. After relaxing for a few minutes, he checked his bleeding foot. There were two deep cuts on the right foot, from the back of the ankle to the heels. He took out his handkerchief and tied it tightly around it. He waited for half an hour, then he decided to climb down and reach his shed, for he had left his cell phone charging in the shed. He decided to stay in the safety of the shed, call for help, and wait until someone came to help him. He fearfully looked around and slowly climbed down the ladder. When he almost crossed the garage, he heard the rustling sound of leaves behind him. He turned around and saw the tiger standing near the fence. He ran immediately to the garage, climbed through the open window, entered the room, and hid behind the boxes. His legs trembled with fear; he cursed himself for climbing down the tank. His leg started to bleed again. Only then did he remember that he had left the window open. He hurried to the window, stuck out his upper body through the opening left for AC, stretched out his right hand, and tried to close the window. The tiger sprung on him from below, got his chest below the arm, and started pulling him out. Since the attack was sudden, his left hand lost its grip, and Muthu fell out of the window. As he fell, his head hit the ground, his neck broke, and his death was instant. The tiger grabbed his body and disappeared.

Muthu's wife became concerned when her repeated calls to her husband went unanswered, so she checked on him on Wednesday. She brought one of her cousins with her. When they arrived, they found the shed empty, and Muthu's cell phone was left charging. They understood that something was wrong and called the police. They also informed

Karuppaiyan, and he, in turn, informed the management. They all came in. The police investigated and concluded that it was a burglary attempt and that the burglars had killed Muthu and disposed of his body.

SEVEN

Maruthu, the elder brother of Keethari Mani, was a widower in his late 40s. He worked as a caretaker in a farmhouse, Valluvar Illam, in Karuppukudi, which was known to the people of the village as Kasan Kadu. He had no one to call family, only his younger brother Mani and his family.

Almost a year after his marriage, Maruthu's wife committed suicide by consuming poison after he went to work in the fields. The previous night, Maruthu, in a fully drunken mood, picked up a quarrel; he gave his wife a hell of a beating. In the morning, his wife pretended to be sleeping since she didn't want to see Maruthu's face. He knew her attitude and behaviour, so he assumed she would recover soon. Since he had urgent work in the fields, he walked out without disturbing her and decided to console her in the afternoon. After he left, she got up and carried out her morning routines. She was in no mood to prepare tea and breakfast.

That was not the first time he drank. Every day, he drank and quarrelled with her, and in the end, she was severely beaten up. It was not just his home but a common scene in the evening in almost every household in Karuppukudi. At the end of the day, the man of the house would visit the liquor shop and reach home in full dose. The irritated wives would pick up a quarrel and get beaten up.

But that day, she thought she had enough of it, so she decided to teach Maruthu a lesson. She got up and walked to the front of the house, where they stored the fertiliser, pesticides, and the sprayer used for pesticides. She pulled out the pesticide, poured it into her mouth, and drank it. She threw the bottle and laid down on the mat.

Maruthu planned to go home in the afternoon, console her, and take her to town; both would have lunch in a restaurant. But fate played its part; his friends took him to the town to buy a sprayer machine, and he managed to return only in the late afternoon. On the way, he grabbed her favourite chicken fried rice from a local eatery and hurriedly reached home.

At home, he found his wife still sleeping, went to the kitchen, and saw no sign of any food. He appreciated his idea of buying the fried rice. He drank a sombu full of water and took the same for his wife. He sat near her to wake her up. When he touched her, her body was unusually chill. He patted her to wake up, but she remained still. When he tried to turn her lifeless face, he was stunned to see the dried foam in her mouth. He wailed so loudly that the entire village gathered in front of his house in no time.

From then on, he lived the life of a widower. For a few years, he continued to work in the fields and looked after his kidai. Then he gave them to his younger brother, Mani, and went to Kerala and Tiruppur to work for a company. He used to come to the festivals, where he worked and how much he earned, no one asked him, and he won't disclose it to anyone. He would bring dresses and other things for his brother's children. When he left for work, he used to hand them some money.

Three years ago, he came and stayed with Mani's family, once and for all. He started to work on the construction sites. Thus, he ended up working on the construction of Velmurugan's farmhouse, Valluvar Illam. There, he came into contact with the Velmurugan. Velmurugan was impressed by the hard work and dedication of Maruthu and offered him a job. He moved in there to maintain the farm. He stayed in the old shed and maintained the farm. He used to visit his brother whenever he found time.

That day, he came to his brother's house to attend the puberty function for his niece. The function went well, and the family had a great day.

After the function, in the late evening at 7.30, Maruthu called, "Mani, it's getting late. I will start."

"Wait, have some food before you go," insisted Mani.

"No... No... I can't eat anymore. Lunch is still in my stomach," replied Maruthu.

"OK, wait, I will pack some sweets for you."

Mani went in, packed some sweets in a carry bag, and gave them to Maruthu. "OK, brother, take care. I will come next week."

"Go carefully. Your cycle doesn't have a light. Why don't you go in the morning?" asked Mani. Maruthu replied, "Vetrivel, sir, will come in the morning. I should go."

He reached for the cloth bag that was folded and clipped to the carrier of his bicycle, slid the carry bag carefully, hung it on the handlebar, and slung it around carefully. He then started his 8-kilometre ride towards Karuppukudi. He peddled along the road. The households in the village had started to settle down for the night. The women were cooking in the *viragu aduppu* outside their homes. The children were still playing on the streets. He rode past them and reached the outskirts of the village. He peddled for around fifteen minutes and reached the Kolathur village, then rode further and came to the outskirts of the village. When he crossed a kilometre, he saw many two-wheelers parked. He looked around and saw many men standing with liquor bottles. A few were sitting on the side of the road, drinking from their bottles and blabbering things. That place was active and busy like *thiruvila*; men from surrounding villages had arrived to drink liquor. In contrast, the village was silent and peaceful.

Maruthu stopped his bicycle in one corner, locked it, and walked to the shop amidst the busy crowd. He approached the counter, stood behind the queue, and waited his turn. When he reached the counter, he bought two-quarter bottles. He tugged the bottles in his *vesti*, walked out, took his bicycle, and started pedalling towards Karuppukudi. He peddled in the darkness, but the two-wheelers that went past him helped him see the road. He reached Karuppukudi, stopped in the shop, and bought a disposal glass and a water bottle. Then he went to an eatery, bought four parottas, an omelette, and one kallaki, moved further down the road towards Palikurichi, and turned right into the mud road. Since it was a familiar road, he rode quickly. After a one-and-a-half-kilometre ride, he reached the farm's fence gate.

He stopped the cycle on the stand and reached into his pocket for the keys. Only then did he remember the bottles, in the *vesti.* He always preferred to drink in open, secluded places. So he decided to finish it before going in to save the trouble of coming back.

There was an open area nearby, parallel to the house and to the right of the muddy road. He rode his bicycle over to it and settled down, placing his bag beside him. The light from the farmhouse provided dim illumination. He then took out his bottles, water bottles, and food parcels. Since his wife's passing, he rarely drank, but he never let others know that he did.

Maruthu opened the bottle, poured the liquor into the glass, added water, and drank in one gulp. Then he opened the parotta parcel, tore the parotta into pieces, poured the chalna on it, mixed it well, and started eating. He sensed something moving behind him in the bushes. He could hear an animal moving through the seemai karuvai bushes. He thought it must be some rats and started concentrating on his glass. He emptied the bottle and felt the kick of the liquor in him. He started eating his food. Again, he heard a faint movement in the bushes. He stood up to check what it was.

As he stood up, the tiger sprung up on him. It knocked him down and bit him in the neck. Instantaneously, his hands held the tiger's jaws firmly. His legs reached the stomach of the tiger. With all his strength and the boost of the liquor, he kicked the tiger. The tiger's flanks tore off from the neck. Blood gushed through the wound, and he gasped for breath. He was breathing through the open wound. He could hear a slight sound when he breathed. He lifted the bicycle and threw it at the tiger. The tiger ran through the bushes. He picked up the cycle again and threw it in the bushes, knelt down, gasping for breath, and held his profoundly bleeding neck.

He rested for a while and stood up to walk. But he fell to the ground and started losing consciousness. His eyesight was fading, and then he saw the face of the tiger, now on the opposite side of the bushes. It casually walked to him. He stumbled, got up, and turned towards the mud road. The tiger threw its front claws; his back was torn like a ribbon from the shoulder to the bottom. He cried in pain, bleeding, and fell to the ground. He tried to get up, but lost all his strength. Tiger lifted him by his right shoulder and carried him away. He was wailing in pain. He carried him through the bushes and seemai karuvai plants. Then it stopped in the bushes and dropped him. His wailing was annoying. He was bleeding and sweating, crying in pain. The tiger buried its flanks and broke his neck. Again, the tiger lifted him and ran deep into the seemai karuvai thicket.

EIGHT

Keelakolathur Forest is located on the fertile banks of the Kolidam in the Ariyalur district of Tamil Nadu. Despite being classified as a forest, it has limited vegetation and wildlife. While it is possible to rarely see a spotted deer, foxes and wild boars are more frequently seen. Velmurugan's house, the Valluvar Illam, was situated on the edge of the Kolathur forest. This stretch of land was previously known as Kasan Kadu and was owned by Alagar's family.

Velmurugan was a farmer who lived in Karuppukudi with his wife, Veni, and two sons, Vetrivel and Vairavel. Vetrivel worked as a superintendent in the Thirumanur union office, while Vairavel worked as a software engineer in Canada. After the death of his wife, Velmurugan wished to settle peacefully on the outskirts of the village and started looking for land. Through one of his friends, he came across Kasan Kadu, the three-acre land owned by Alagar. At first, Velmurugan was hesitant due to the distance from the village. However, the price offered by Alagar was meagre and irresistible, so he decided to buy it. Initially, Alagar offered half of the land to Velmurugan to marry off his daughter. Then, within two years, Alagar sold the entire land to Velmurugan and sent his son abroad.

The plot of land was a perfect rectangle, measuring 650 feet in length and 200 feet in breadth. It was located almost two kilometres away from the main road, and the only way to reach it was by taking the mud road that deviated from the Karuppukudi to the Palikurichi main road. The neighbouring lands were donated to temples, but most of them were abandoned and uncultivated. These lands were supposed to be leased out for cultivation. The lands adjacent to Valluvar Illam were also temple lands that were left uncultivated. Thick seemai karuvai plants grew in abundance there.

Velmurugan and Vetrivel often approached the concerned people to clear the plants, but their efforts went in vain. So Velmurugan and his sons made it a point to keep the fences in place. They used green poly mesh in the fence, from the ground to a height of two feet, to keep unwanted creatures from entering the land. The land was kept free from bushes and unwanted shrubs. so that the children could roam all over the three acres of land without fear. Alagar worked on the land; he planted coconut, teak, mangoes, and neem trees and grew vegetables and other plants for home use.

After a couple of years, Velmurugan decided to build a house, live there, and take care of the trees. However, everyone, including his sons, objected to his idea. Despite their objections, he went ahead with the construction.

The house was constructed with a 30 x 60 proportion and had three floors. It was surrounded by a five-foot-high compound wall with a sliding gate. The ground floor was designed for parking, similar to that of an apartment, with only pillars and no walls. Velmurugan's sons thought it was unnecessary since the cars could be parked anywhere inside the fence. However, Velmurugan convinced them that it would prevent burglars from accessing the windows. The first and second floors of the building were intended for residential use. An external staircase from the parking area was used to access the first floor. The landing of this staircase had a balcony, and Velmurugan insisted on installing a heavy grill with a gate that opened to the stairs to provide added security against burglars. Additionally, a heavy gate was fitted to the back door. The CCTV cameras and inverters powered by solar panels were also installed.

Despite taking all necessary precautions, the security of the house was put to the test when it was burgled during the COVID-19 lockdown. Velmurugan, his two sons, and their families had moved to the farmhouse as a safety measure against the virus. One night, the whole family was sleeping in their respective bedrooms, and Velmurugan was sleeping on the sofa in the hall. Maruthu went to stay with his brother's family for a couple of days, and the family was left alone.

In the middle of the night, Velmurugan woke up suddenly, unsure of what had disturbed his sleep. He sat on the sofa and closed his eyes, thinking that old age had brought him many sleepless nights. As he tried to calm his mind and drift off, he heard the sound of metal in the silence of the night. Soon, he realised the sound had come from the gate. It sounded like someone was shaking the gate violently. He searched for his phone and found it in the corner of the sofa. After sliding his finger to unlock it, he opened the camera app. The CCTV cameras around his house were connected online, allowing him to monitor them from anywhere. He selected the camera for the front gate and was shocked to see three men standing there. Their faces were covered with winter *Kullas*. One of them had his hand through one of the gaps in the gate, holding a rod and trying to break the lock. The force of his effort shook the gate violently, disturbing Velmurugan's sleep.

Velmurugan realised the danger that his family was in. Meanwhile, he observed that the men at the gates had understood that the lock would not open. As he watched through the camera, the man who had attempted to break the lock handed over the rod and began to saw the padlock with a hacksaw blade. He immediately called 100 to inform the police and contacted a few of his friends from the village. However, help in any form would take at least half an hour to reach them. He then woke up the family members. He was sure the padlock and the teak double door wouldn't stop them. The family needed fifteen to twenty minutes, at the least, to get any help from the villagers. But the front teak door would not hold that long. A quick decision was to be made.

Vetrivel said, "Appa, we have to leave. The doors won't hold, and they'll enter the house for sure." Vairavel said, "We can go to the terrace and lock the back door and gate behind us. They won't be able to reach the steps. Let them take whatever they want and leave." Velmurugan thought the idea was good, so he didn't wait for anyone. He opened the back door and the gate, and without making a sound, everyone left the house and climbed the stairs. Vairavel quickly went back into the house and grabbed two spare locks from the cupboard. He locked the wooden door behind him and then the gate. They all made it to the terrace and waited.

They used their cell phones connected online to the cameras to monitor the movements of the burglars. The burglars were now working on the wooden door, and in a few minutes, they would be inside. Velmurugan called his friends and the police again. Now Vairavel had an idea: "Let us trap them inside the house." "But how?" asked the father. Vetrivel replied, "He is correct. We can use the locks from the compound gate and lock the balcony gates from outside." "They will break that lock, too," said Velmurugan. "Yes. They will. But it will buy us some time. Before they break the lock, our friends and the police will be here.," replied Vairavel. "But if they see you locking the gates, you will be in danger." "Appa, it is more dangerous if they come around and find us here. So, let us take the risk." They checked the cameras; by now, the door had given in, and the burglars had entered the house. Now, Vairavel and Vetrivel quickly grabbed the aluminium ladder and climbed down the stairs. They carefully climbed down the ladder from the stairway to the ground floor. They walked to the front and hid behind their cars. Vetrivel pulled out the phone and saw that the burglars were searching the bedrooms. One of them opened the first bedroom door. The brothers quickly reacted without wasting time.

Vairavel signalled his brother to watch the cameras and warn him. He unlocked the compound gate, took the lock, tiptoed to the balcony door, and locked it from outside. Vairavel saw the burglars moving around the house. They were thoroughly shocked to see that the house was empty. Then they climbed downstairs and checked all the rooms and the kitchen again. Then they went to the back door and found it closed from outside. They were shocked and rushed to the front door. They were stunned to see the gate locked from the outside with a new lock. It was chaos—a mixture of shouting, abusing, and threatening. One of them said, "I suggested someone stay back to watch the door. You thought I was trying to escape. Look what happened." "Now's not the right time to regret it. Break the lock!" shouted the other one. One of them reached the lock and used the rod to break it. The taller of them shouted at him, "Are you mad? You know that the lock won't break... Use the hacksaw blade, idiot." That man dropped the rod and took the hacksaw blade. The tall man shouted, "Hey, we know you are all hiding here. Open the lock, we won't hurt you; we will leave the place... Hey, come out... Do you hear me? Or else we will set the house on fire. Come out." He used all the abusive terms available in Tamil. The other man urged the man sawing the lock, "Do it fast....". Unfortunately, that man dropped the hacksaw blade. It fell on the stairs, and he could not reach it. Now, his companions went wild. They started abusing him and threatened to kill him.

All three finally realised nothing could be done and sat on the floor. Just then, the villagers from Karuppukudi arrived in two-wheelers. Then, the police patrol and police personnel came in. Vairavel and Vetrivel handed the key to the police. They opened the lock and arrested the three. They removed the *kulla* that covered their faces, and the villagers were not surprised to see Alagar and his friends. Vairavel took the key, went behind the house, and threw it to his father. Velmurugan opened the back gates and came out through the front gate of the house. He was shocked to see Alagar. The word he uttered was "*throgi*". The police took them in their vehicles, and Vetrivel and Vairavel followed them in the car.

After this incident, safety provisions in that house were doubled. Two steel gates were added in the front and behind the main door. The double door was replaced by a single teak door with mechanical deadbolt locks installed in it. Another steel safety door was added to the back door. The front balcony door was welded with shutter locks. The house was fitted with high-capacity solar panels, and more cameras were added around the fence. All these works were done to the fullest satisfaction of Velmurugan. Many of his friends advised him to sell the house. But he firmly stayed in the house with his family until he died in a couple of years.

After his father's death, Vetrivel moved to a rented house in Thirumanur, leaving the house in the hands of Maruthu. Maruthu took care of the house and the three-acre property. Vetrivel's family used to spend weekends and holidays at the house. The trees on the property started to grow fast in the capable hands of Maruthu. After Velmurugan's death, both Vetrivel and Vairavel's families would spend their vacation here and explore the surrounding area together with Maruthu.

NINE

Soundar comes from Velankudi, a village located three kilometres south of Karuppukudi. He is a skilled electrician and plumber with experience working on many construction sites. After completing his ITI, he started as an assistant and gained expertise in wiring and plumbing. He got married at the age of twenty and fathered a boy at the age of twenty-one and a girl the following year. As his family grew, he found it challenging to make ends meet. Therefore, he took a loan by pledging his land as collateral and worked in Saudi Arabia for nine years. After he returned to his village, he purchased four acres of land and a few cattle and built a new house where he and his family could settle down and live comfortably.

Soundar started his career as a plumber for construction sites in villages and areas around Ariyalur. He was then hired to work on Velmurugan's house and quickly gained his trust through his dedication and hard work. After that, Velmurugan relied solely on him for any electrical or plumbing work required. With more experience, he began taking on bigger buildings and more complex projects.

Soundar met Ponni, a twenty-five-year-old sithal, at one of the construction sites he was working at. Ponni had left her husband because he was an intolerant drunkard who wasn't earning enough. She was living alone with her four-year-old son in a rented house. Soundar and Ponni developed a liking and started seeing each other in secret. However, people started to talk about their relationship, and their affair became more serious when Soundar began spending the night at Ponni's house.

Meanwhile, his wife, Pavunu, started to hear about her husband's affair and started quarrelling with him. As the days went on, the quarrel intensified. One day, Pavunu and her son Ravi went to Ponni's house and made quite a scene. Ravi almost hit her and vandalised her house. The house owner of Ponni strictly told her to vacate the house. So, she was compelled to move her house to the next village. Soundar helped her shift the house. Now, Ponni got fed up with the events and started nagging Soundar that he had brought disgrace to her. To escape the heat of the situation, Soundar started drinking. His son was very adamant and arrogant in dealing with his father's affair. Once, he went to the extent of making posters about his father's affair with Ponni and pasting them in both villages where they lived. Soundar started drinking throughout the day and started staying with Ponni. Gradually, his concentration on work decreased, and he agreed to work on only a few selected buildings.

Things got heated up when Soundar stopped going home and stayed with Ponni. However, his son, Ravi, was not willing to give up and went straight to her home and started shouting and abusing them. Ponni couldn't take it and started shouting and insulting Soundar. So Soundar started staying at the construction sites he worked at and carried out his work. Since he stopped visiting Ponni, there was a lull in his life for a few days. It was in this situation that Vetrivel called him to repair the damages in the drainage pipes, install a few more cameras, and replace the DVX. Meanwhile, Ponni's present house owner urged her to vacate the house, and this time, he decided to lease a house in a distant village. So, to pay the lease amount, he closed the fixed deposit he had for two lakhs and gave it to Ponni.

Ravi was angered, and after a visit to the liquor shop, he went straight to the construction site where Soundar was staying and started a heated quarrel. Since both were drunk, the quarrel ended in fighting. Both started beating up each other, and Ravi went further and started destroying Soundar's belongings, including his motorcycle, cell phones, and tools.

The villagers gathered around and tried to pacify them before they brought them under control. A lot of damage was done to Soundar, his belongings, and the articles on the new construction site. Once the people around him left him, Soundar walked into the house and fell asleep.

Soundar woke suddenly, opening his eyes to find himself lying on a mat. It was late morning, and he felt pain all over his body. He remembered the work ahead of him and the call he had received from Vetrivel the day before. Despite having a deadline to finish his current project, Soundar knew that Vetrivel would not allow any other electrician to touch his work. Vetrivel had promised to reach the farmhouse by 11:00 a.m. So, he must reach the farmhouse in Karuppukudi on time. He noticed a few bruises and the torn shirt as he glanced at himself. His mind recalled the fight he had with his son the previous night. He searched for his cell phone, but all he found was a curved, shattered object that used to be his phone.

As he stepped outside, he found his motorcycle lying on the ground. The front wheel was beyond repair due to a rock thrown at it by his son from the nearby construction site. He slowly knelt down beside his damaged bike, contemplating how much his life had changed. He was aware that the mistake was on him, but he didn't know how to fix it.

He decided to visit Vetrivel and then continue working at the site. Since his assistant had not arrived, he estimated he had about an hour to get ready. He got up, went outside to refresh himself, returned, bathed, changed his torn clothes, and started to wait for his assistant. He planned to use his assistant's bike while his assistant continued with the previous day's work. Just then, Soundar's friend Prakash arrived to check on him after the events of the previous night. Prakash offered Soundar consolation and advice. During their conversation, Prakash mentioned that he had a job in Melaiyur and was about to leave. Soundar informed Prakash that he also had work in Karuppukudi and asked him to drop by Karuppukudi. He got off at the bridge on the Karuppukudi and Melaiyur roads.

Soundar waited patiently on the road for a lift to the mud road, and then from there, he intended to walk to the farmhouse. After a ten-minute wait, he saw a motorcycle coming his way; he stopped it and asked the rider, "Can you drop me on the mud road?" The man replied, "I am going to the farmhouse. If you want, you can come with me to that house. My name is Mani, and my brother Maruthu works there." "Oh, I am the electrician. Soundar, I am also going to the farm house, Vetrivel, sir; the owner asked for immediate help with repairs. Where is Maruthu? Is he staying with you in your house?" The man replied, "No. My brother came back on Monday night. He did not turn up for Nalleer, and his phone was switched off, so I came to check on him." Soundar climbed the pillion and said, "Ok, let us go. Sir will be waiting. We will discuss on the way." They rode to the outskirts, took the mud road, and proceeded on it.

TEN

Nalleru pootuthal is a ceremony celebrated by the farmers of Tamil Nadu on the first day of the Tamil month of *Chithirai*. The first day of *Chithirai* marks the beginning of the Tamil New Year. It usually falls on April 14. Farmers plough their lands that day and prepare them for that year's cultivation.

On April 14, the Tamil New Year is celebrated in a completely different way compared to January 1. There are no cake-cutting or midnight parties or celebrations. Instead, people in Tamil Nadu visit their family deities and temples to pray for a good beginning of the coming year. This is a traditional way of celebrating the Tamil New Year and is deeply rooted in the culture of the people of Tamil Nadu.

Apart from his Kidai, Mani owned about five acres of land in Aravakurichi, which he cultivated with the help of his wife. This also included his share, his elder brother Maruthu's share, and the two acres of land he had purchased near his land. Every year, Mani would take a break from Kidai for a day or two to celebrate Naller, and his elder brother Maruthu would join him.

Mani had made all the arrangements the previous evening. He cleaned the old wooden *yer kalapai* that was kept aside safely for this purpose. It had been handed down through the generations. Though the tractors replaced the wooden *yer kalapai* and the bulls, farmers kept a wooden *yer kalapai* for this day. He checked it for damages and cleaned it.

On April 14, Mani woke up to the sound of his wife, Malini, shouting at the children, "Hey, children, get up and take a bath. Periyappa will be here. We should not be late to the temple." The children lazily stood up and went out to finish their morning routine. Mani sat up on his mat and asked his wife, "Have you packed the things needed in the temple? Annan will be here any minute." "You don't have to worry. Everything is set and ready. Please get yourself ready, and the children will be ready soon," replied his wife. He went out and came back after half an hour. By the time the children were almost ready, his daughter, Deepa, was doing her long, pretty hair.

The whole family got ready to leave for the temple in half an hour. However, they had to wait for Maruthu. Mani tried calling Maruthu, but his phone was switched off. Mani wondered why his brother's phone was off and grew impatient as he looked at the clock, thinking about what could be the reason for Maruthu's delay. Malini said, "It's getting late. We better go to the temple. We should prepare pongal. If we get delayed in the temple, we will be late for Nalleru. If Mama comes and finds that we are gone, he will understand the situation and come straight to the temple." His wife sounded correct. So, Mani and his family left for the temple, half-hearted.

They all reached the temple of *Madurai Veran,* their family deity. The temple was crowded. Malini said, "Look at the crowd. Half of the village is here. We should have come earlier. I will find a spot to prepare pongal." The children joined her. Mani came out of the crowd and tried to reach Maruthu's phone again, then joined the other men. His friends and relatives started asking about his brother, and he told them he would be there any minute. But his mind told him something was wrong. He began contemplating various reasons for his brother's absence. He recollected the events that took place during his daughter's function and wondered if his wife had said or done something that offended him. In the meantime, his wife prepared the Pongal. However, due to the large number of people waiting to perform *padaiyal*, they had to wait for their turn.

After a long wait, it was their turn to offer prayers to their family deity. They spread a *thalai valai ilai* before the idol. They laid out the offerings of *pongal, pori, pottukadalai, aval, vellam, vetrilai, pakku*, banana, and coconut. Once they had completed the ritual, the leaf was taken, and they made way for others. They sat near the temple and shared the pongal and pori that had been offered to God. However, Maruthu was still missing, and Mani thought that he might be waiting at home.

The family reached home to find that Maruthu hadn't turned up. They all sat down to eat their breakfast. Then it was time for *Naller*, so he took his *yer kalapai* and bulls and walked with the family to the Amman temple. The family joined the other families of the farmers from the village. Soon, the prayer was started, and all the *yer kalapai* and the bulls were worshipped, and they started to plough the temple land. Then Mani took his *yer kalapai* and bulls to his land, and his family followed him. On the way, he called the tractor that he had already hired. They all reached the land, and again, Mani offered prayers to his *yer kalapai*, bull, and tractor. Then he started to plough the land with his *yer kalapai* and bull, and the tractor followed them. Mani ploughed the land for some time, and then the tractor did the rest of the ploughing.

Though he was busy throughout the day, his mind was obsessed with the absence of Maruthu. Mani waited for his brother's arrival. He tried to reach his brother over the phone, but the phone was switched off. He was also not familiar with his brother's friends in Karuppukudi. He was worried about his brother since he was alone in the farmhouse. Even if he got sick, no one would know it. So, he decided to go in person and see for himself.

The following day was a Saturday. After completing his work, he had a late breakfast and rode on his motorcycle to Karuppukudi, arriving at 1.00 p.m. After inquiring about his brother with his friends, he discovered that he had been absent for at least a week. Then he rode towards the farmhouse; when he reached the school, A stranger stopped him on the main road, near the bridge, and asked for a lift. "Can you drop me on the mud road?" Mani replied, "I am going to the farmhouse. If you want, you can come with me to that house. My brother Maruthu works there." "Oh. I am the electrician, Soundar. I am also going to the farmhouse, Vetrivel, sir; the owner asked for immediate help with repairs. Where is Maruthu? Is he staying with you in your house?" Mani replied, "No. My brother came back on Monday night. He did not turn up for Naller, and his phone was switched off, so I came to check on him." Soundar climbed the pillion and said, "Ok, let us go. Sir is waiting. We will discuss on the way." They rode to the outskirts, took the mud road, and proceeded on it.

When they took the last turn, they heard a loud growl from the bushes to their left. Immediately, they turned their heads around, and a tiger jumped on Soundar. Mani lost his balance, the motorcycle fell to the right, and Mani fell along with the motorcycle. In the meantime, Soundar was dislodged and taken into the air by the tiger. The tiger and Soundar rolled down to the vaikal on the right side of the road. Mani was dragged by the motorcycle, and it banged at a tree. He fell into the vaikal on the left side of the road. He started to bleed from the cut on the head and couldn't move a muscle. He almost missed the seemai karuvai plants and lodged in the gap between the two young plants of seemai karuvai.

Mani attempted to stand up, but in a moment of weakness, he noticed Soundar stumbling down the vaikal. Mani wanted to call out to him for help, but he couldn't move. He lay there motionless. After a few minutes of silence, he spotted a tiger following Soundar's trail. Mani realised that perhaps Soundar and the tiger had fallen down the vaikal and rolled. The tiger may have been injured and was watching Soundar from a distance. Once Soundar regained his composure and started walking, the tiger must have wanted its prey. He was happy that he was tucked between the bushes. The tiger couldn't see him and decided to take Soundar. He fainted when he started to wonder if it was the same tiger he encountered in Ullur.

When Mani regained consciousness, he saw two men standing beside him. One of them splashed water on his face and asked him what happened, while the other kept a watch on the surroundings. It was only then that Mani noticed that both men had guns. The man who had splashed water on his face helped him to stand up, and Mani said, "A tiger attacked me." The man then helped Mani climb the mud road, and together, they made their way to the house.

ELEVEN

On Saturday, Vetrivel woke up early in the morning. He called out to his wife, Thenmozhi, "Have you prepared breakfast? It's getting late. Soundar will be waiting for me. He has some other work to do. He will be on his way once I show him the damage and the things to be repaired. Marthu's cell phone is switched off. I tried to call him yesterday. I don't know what happened to his phone. Maybe something happened to him." "He will be perfectly alright. His phone might have been damaged. Your breakfast is ready," replied his wife. Vetrivel sat down to eat his breakfast and said to his wife, "I will try to finish the work as soon as possible. If I am unable to complete it today, I will stay back and leave by tomorrow afternoon after giving instructions to Maruthu and Soundar."

Vetrivel's brother would visit them every year in May, and they would all spend a month at the farmhouse. Vetrivel had to ensure everything was in order and prepare the house for the month-long stay. His brother and family would join them for their summer vacation. Vetrivel packed all the groceries and other necessary items he had bought for the month's stay, as well as the list of things Maruthu had given him previously. He checked that the DVX he had bought to replace the damaged one at Karuppukudi's house was working fine. After loading everything onto his motorcycle, he set off for his farmhouse in Karuppukudi.

He arrived at the compound gate of Valluvar Illam at 11:00 a.m. and was surprised to find that the area had been unattended for at least a week. He proceeded to open the gate and walk in, only to find that the ground was entirely covered with dry leaves. He noticed animal droppings scattered here and there and wondered what kind of animal could have entered the fenced area. He decided to check the fence for any damages and rode his motorcycle inside the compound gate. The floor was covered with dust and sand, so he climbed up the dusty stairs and opened the gate and door of the house. After that, he went down, picked up the bundles from his motorcycle, and placed them on the table.

He took out his phone and called Soundar, but his phone was switched off. Wondering what might have happened to Soundar's phone, he kept his phone in his pants pocket, took the vacuum cleaner, and started cleaning. He first cleaned the hall and the rooms on the first floor, then the rooms on the second floor, and mopped the floors.

When he started cleaning the furniture, he heard someone yelling outside in agony and fear. "Sir! Sir! Please save me.... Pulli is chasing to kill me." He couldn't understand the words. He walked to the window and saw Soundar on the mud road, almost dragging towards the compound gate; his right hand was visibly broken and hanging, and his right leg was also broken. He understood something was wrong, rushed out of the house, climbed downstairs, opened the compound gate, and ran into the open space to help him.

Vetrivel shouted back as he ran to the gate, "Soundar, what happened to you? I don't understand what you say. Did you fall or have an accident?" When Vetrivel was just thirty feet away from the gate, Soundar had already reached it and was struggling to open the latch on top. Then, suddenly, they both heard the growl of a tiger. Soundar frantically beat the gate and held on to it firmly. But the tiger sprang from the vaikal nearby and grabbed him as he cried in fear and agony. His cries echoed around the place. The tiger grabbed him, slung him across its back, and disappeared into the forest at the same speed it came. Vetrivel stopped abruptly, tumbled, fell, and rolled on the ground. He came to a stop and lay on the ground. Vetrivel couldn't believe what he just saw. He recollected himself and started running back to the house as fast as he could.

Vetrivel reached the compound gate of the house, closed it and bolted it, fell on the stairs, and rested a while, hissing and puffing like a steam engine. Again, he climbed the stairs at full speed, closed the gate, and latched behind him. After resting there for a while, he went inside the home, brought a lock, and locked it, then went inside and locked the door and the safety gate. Then he rushed to the back door that took him to the terrace staircase, locked that gate, the door, and then the safety gate. Then he walked to the sofa, fell on it, and started crying loudly.

He then gradually recalled the scene that happened before him. He couldn't believe that a tiger lived in that area. He knew that it was the edge of the Kulathur forest. But there was no thick vegetation, and wild animals such as foxes, wild boars, hares, and a few spotted deer were always a rare sight. They had been to the forest several times, along with the children. He was sure there were no predatory animals in the area. He had not heard about them from his father or grandfather. So, the thought of a tiger or a leopard in the Kolathur forest had never occurred to him or the villagers.

Vetrivel realised what might have happened to Maruthu. His cell phone was switched off for around a week, so he must have been killed one week ago. He decided to inform the police and searched for his cell phone. It was not in his pocket. He searched all over the hall. Then he realised that it might have fallen to the ground. He wanted to get the cell phone. But the thought of going out and looking for it frightened him. He waited for some time and realised that no one could help him unless he called them. There were very few chances that people could come this way, so he had to get his phone, call the police, and get help.

He carefully opened the front door of the house, stood on the balcony, and scanned the ground for his cell phone. He found it in the place where he fell down. The thought of stepping out of the house frightened him, but he needed the cell phone to call for help. He prayed to his *Kula theivam*, Karuppaiyan, and called the spirits of his father to help him. He slowly opened the gate, stepped out, stood on the staircase, glanced around, quickly climbed down the stairs, stopped at the last stair, and glanced around the compound again. Then he opened the compound gate inch by inch. The compound gate would make a screech, so he opened it only to allow him to squeeze through. He stopped when his body was halfway through the gate. He stood still, legs trembling, with sweat running all over his body. He looked at the surroundings, near the teak tree rows and the coconut trees that lined the border of the fence, as well as the back and sides of the outhouse where Maruthu stayed.

Then, gathering courage and with a shuddering heart, he cautiously approached the cell phone, careful not to make any noise. Constantly glancing towards the bushes beyond the fence, which stood about 100 feet away, he couldn't help but curse his neighbours for not maintaining their lands properly. Finally, he reached the spot, picked up the phone, and got the shock of his life. The phone was broken. His phone had slipped from his pocket and was shattered when he fell to the ground.

He stood there looking at the phone for a few seconds, forgetting all about the tiger. He felt like crying and was sorry for putting it in his pocket. He decided to leave the place immediately. He ran to the house, locked it, climbed down, and took his motorcycle out. When he was about to lock the compound gate, he saw three men walking towards the fence gate. Two of them had guns, and the other was limping and injured.

TWELVE

In the first week of April, Arul and Viji decided to go after the tiger and finish what they started. Both were discharged from the hospital ten days after the accident, and one whole month of treatment and rest had restored strength in them. The wounds and cuts on their heads had healed completely. It was sad that Kolanji didn't survive the accident. He died on the way to the hospital.

After their discharge from the hospital, they checked for news about the activity of the tiger in newspapers and on TV. They expected the tiger to be somewhere in the districts of Ariyalur or Thanjavur. They received the news of a tiger attack in Ullur, in Ariyalur district. But then they were not strong enough to go after it. Now fully recovered from the injuries, they decided to go after the tiger. They want to put an end to what they have initiated. Arul repeatedly told Viji, "The tiger would become a danger to people if it could not find food in the forest. It would take the cattle from the villages. It was already a cattle lifter. It would encounter man; if it tasted the human flesh and learned that humans are easy to kill, it would become a man-eater. Imagine a man-eater killing people in an area where the people haven't even imagined a tiger roaming in their area. We must get it. We should either catch it alive or kill it."

They heard nothing about the tiger throughout March. Both were worried. They would be happy if the tiger was dead, but it would be very dangerous if it was still in that area. It had walked around 80 km from the place of the accident to Ullur. From there, it could have travelled in any direction, and in one month, it could have reached anywhere. However, they had no other option but to wait.

One afternoon at the end of March, Viji brought a two-week-old newspaper: "There is news of a girl missing in a village named Karuppukudi, in Ariyalur District. She was missing while grazing her cattle," Viji gave the newspaper to Arul. Arul questioned, "What was the reason given for missing?" "Police say that the girl was missing under mysterious circumstances. But the people say that the girl eloped with her lover. But the father of the girl did not accept it." "What is your opinion?" asked Arul. Viji continued, "Karuppukudi is just 29 km from Ullur. This village is also near Kolathur Forest. I am afraid it could be our tiger. It might have turned into a man-eater. What do you say?" Arul thought awhile, "You could be correct, but elopement is very common nowadays. We should check on the situation in person. If it had turned into a man-eater, we should kill it. People should not die for our mistakes. Tomorrow, we will go to Karuppukudi and check the situation." Viji nodded and turned to walk out. "Viji, pack some dresses and take everything needed. If you were correct, we would need them; we should finish the tiger." Viji walked out, and Arul sat thoughtfully.

The next day, by early morning, they were on their way to Karuppukudi. They reached Karuppukudi by 3:00 p.m. in the afternoon. They reached a lonely tea shop in that village, ordered tea, and started enquiring with the shop owner. Arul did the talking while Viji watched them silently. "There was news about a girl missing from the village. Where is her house?" The shop owner handed them the tea glasses and said, "Fourth street on the left... last house in that street. Are you policemen?" "Yes," replied Arul. "Has she eloped with someone, or is there any other reason for her disappearance?" The man said, "As far as I know, the girl is good. But there is an old saying: *entha ponthula entha pambu irrukumnu yaruku therium* (Who knows which snake will be in which pond?). Plus, there is no other reason behind the disappearance of a girl. Everyone in the village knows she is a good girl, but the boys somehow spoil their minds, sir." "It seems the girl was missing while grazing the cattle. Where is that place?". "If you walk on this road, you will see a school on your left; next to the school, you will see a road towards the east; next to that, there is a Yeri; if you walk further for half a kilometre, you will see a mud road towards the west; if you walk on that road for one-and-a-half kilometres, you will see a small bridge with a pungai tree; under that bridge, they found her things. It seems that she had asked her man to come there, and from there, they escaped. By this time, they might have gotten married and settled."

Arul and Viji handed the tea glasses and the money and walked in the direction the shopkeeper said. They walked past the school and then the yeri. When they reached the mud road, a man rushed in on a two-wheeler and said, "Ayya, vanakam, I am Ilakiyaa's father. The tea shopkeeper sent me a boy to inform me that the police were inquiring about my daughter. He also told me that you were walking to the spot. So, I came rushing to meet you. I will show the place, sir."

Arul and Viji stared at each other. Arul thought that they shouldn't have affirmed when the shopkeeper asked if they were police. They continued to walk further. The girl's father parked the motorcycle on the side of the road. All three walked up to the bridge and then climbed down. Then the father showed them the place where they found her things. The father firmly said, "I know my daughter very well. The villagers had defamed her and my family, sir. Someone had abducted her. Please find my daughter, sir." He started crying; they consoled him, got his cellphone number, and sent him home.

Once the man reached the road and took his two-wheeler, they climbed the mud road, stood on the bridge, and looked around. The mud road ran further west and then turned right. The mud road was open only for around 100 feet. Beyond that, it was covered with palm, pungai, thungumunchi, and neem trees. Mostly, the area was covered by seemai karuvai in all shapes and sizes. From there, they could see the top floor of a lonely house in the deep, far interior of this growth.

In front of them stood a lonely pungai tree a hundred feet away. Behind them was open land stretching south towards the main road. There, the cattle of the missing girl were grazing. The police must have scanned that area. So, they decided to check the land before them. Arul instructed Viji, "It's been more than ten days, so look at the ground carefully." They spread out and started scanning the ground towards the tree. Arul scanned around the tree and found dark spots big and small all over the place, a few blue beads worn by girls, and blood-stained bits of red cloth with green leaves printed on them. "Viji, look at these dark spots. It must be blood. Things are happening as we guessed. Now we should confirm the beads and clothes belong to the girl."

Arul pulled out his phone from his pocket and called the girl's father. "We are the police, and we need some details for our report. What dress was your girl wearing, and was she wearing any beads on the neck?" He listened silently to the voice. "Viji, you are correct. It is the girl; the tiger turned into a man-eater and started to kill in daylight." "Arul, we should warn everyone." "They will ask us how we know about it." Both started thinking silently. Arul looked at the ground and said to Viji, "Check for blood trails." Both started examining the ground. Viji said, "No blood trail. Did it eat the girl here?" "No, pieces of bone will be here. It looks like no one, not even the police, checked this spot, said Arul. "It was not their mistake; they might not have imagined that a tiger would be roaming in this area. We have to wait until something happens. No other go." He pointed to the thick growth in the direction of that lonely house. "I think the tiger is in that area. We must warn the people in the building. I have never seen people living in such lonely places." Viji reminded him, "We are losing light; we should go back, and we will come in daylight and warn them. It's dangerous to stand here. Let's go." Arul remarked, "Tiger did not have enough food, so it risks and takes man in daylight. Come, let's go."

They walked hurriedly, looking around. Arul said, "It is our luck that the tiger is still operating on the outskirts of the village. We barely have a week before the tiger expands its territory and enters the village. If we manage to bag it before that, we can avoid unwanted scenes." Viji nodded his head.

Arul and Viji reached the main road and saw people driving their cattle home. When they reached the school, they saw two boys sitting on the deserted school veranda. They were shocked to see them there and rushed to them. "What are you doing here? It is getting dark. Why don't you go home?" One of the boys pointed to the kitchen building of the school and said, "We are waiting for Thatha. We came to see if he had come today. We come here daily by this time and leave before dark." "Why? Where is he now?" asked Viji. "Don't know; we haven't seen him since last Monday. He used to sleep here. Morning, he will go and come back in the evening." "Ok, it's getting dark. You should go." They took the kids with them. The kids told them the story of the old man. They waited on the main road until the boys safely entered their streets and then their homes.

Arul and Viji walked silently towards their jeep. Viji said, "I think the tiger took the old man too." "Mmm….. We should check in the morning before someone comes." Viji suggested, "Shall we stay in the school tonight and check the area around it before anyone knows?". "Sure, if we are lucky, we may get the tiger. Or else we can guard the passersby on the road," affirmed Arul. They drove the Jeep towards Palikurichi and had their dinner. They returned after 10:00 p.m.

They reached the school, parked the jeep near the compound, and took out two bags. Arul unpacked his thermal binoculars and scanned the area. After making sure everything was fine, they walked to the three-classroom building. Arul handed his bag to Viji and climbed the building, using the sun shade of the window near the odai and the kitchen. Then Viji handed both bags and climbed next.

They went to the corner of the terrace and cleaned it. The terrace was open without a side wall. Arul took the first turn of the watch. Viji lay on the cleaned surface of the terrace and dozed off. Arul took out his tranquilliser gun and thermal binoculars and started looking out. He sat away from the corner to avoid slipping off in the darkness. Only a few vehicles moved around, mostly two-wheelers. He worried that if the tigers took one of them, everyone would know about the tiger. Before things happened, he wanted to finish it off. He lay on his stomach and started watching, but the tiredness overtook him, and he slept in a few minutes.

When he woke up, Viji was watching; he took out his phone. The time was two in the morning. "I will check the other sides." Arul took out his things, walked to the other edge, and started looking through the thermal imaging binoculars. He carefully checked on all sides, then walked back to Viji, laid down, and closed his eyes. His mind was thinking about his plans for the next day.

Then he heard the sound—the familiar sound of an animal moving through the twigs and bushes. He opened his eyes and saw that Viji was not looking in the direction in which the sound came. For a second, he thought it was his imagination, but he continued to hear the sound. But Viji was not hearing it. He gave Viji a gentle nudge on his elbow. Viji turned around, and Arul pointed out the direction. Only then did Viji realise his mistake and pick up his binoculars. While Arul reached for his binoculars, Viji dropped his binoculars, took his tranquilliser gun, and looked through the scope. He saw the tiger moving through the seemai karuvai bushes. In excitement, Viji took a hurried shot. Arul looked in that direction. The dart missed the tiger because of the twigs and bushes. It hit the twig just above the shoulder of the tiger and fell down. The tiger got irked by the sound and took off. In one bounce, it climbed onto the road, crossed it, and ran towards the forest. "Why are you shooting when you know you can't hit it?" Arul was mad at Viji. Viji was very sorry for what he did. Arul continued, "We are responsible for what is happening here. We are here to correct it. Please get off with it and use your brain. Concentration and patience are very important for people like us." Viji listened to him with closed eyes. "Pack the things and get some sleep; in the morning, we should check that lonely house." Arul lay on the terrace, and soon Viji joined him. Both dozed off.

At first light, they climbed down, loaded the bags in the jeep, and went to the odai behind the kitchen. There was no water, so it was covered with Seema karuvai. Arul carefully looked for the broken dart and picked it up. They climbed the road and saw a vesti tangled in karuvai thorns. Viji removed it. "Must be the old man's clothes, so two kills." They walked along the road for some distance. Then they went to the Yeri, bathed in the water tank opposite the school, and drove off to Palikurichi for breakfast.

After lunch, Arul and Viji were back in Karuppukudi at 2 o'clock. This time, they crossed the village and parked the jeep near the mud road. Arul wanted to take the Jeep off the road to avoid suspicions among the people. But he decided to take it in after checking the mud road. So, they left the Jeep on the main road.

They took out their .12 shotgun, checked it, released the safety, put it inside the cover, held it with the cover for ready use, and started walking towards the lonely house. After a thirty-minute walk, they almost reached the house. Arul wondered what made them build such a big house in this place, but the place was beautiful and green with trees. When they reached the last turn, they heard the wailing of a man, surely a cry of pain and agony. Both took the rifles from the cover and started running in that direction. After taking the last turn, they saw a motorcycle lying on the road. Arul said, "It must be an accident." They ran towards the motorcycle, but no one was found near it. They checked around, and Viji found a middle-aged man lying on the left side of Vaikal. They tried to wake him, but he was unconscious.

Arul instructed Viji to splash water on his face, and then he climbed on the mud road and stood guard with his rifle. Viji splashed water on the man's face. When the man gained consciousness, Viji helped him to stand up, and they slowly climbed towards Arul. "Did he say anything, Viji?" asked Arul. "Nothing much. He just said a tiger attacked him. He is in shock. He didn't talk much. Let us take him to the house." The man was severely wounded in the head, left shoulder, and legs but readily walked with them. Viji helped him, and Arul walked behind them with his rifle ready. Arul wondered if this man was unconscious and then who made the sound. They reached the fence gate of the house. The stone on it read, 'Valluvar Illam'.

THIRTEEN

Vetrivel stood confused as the three men opened the fence gate and made their way into the compound, two of them leading and one following, and all three were scanning their surroundings. One of the men appeared to have a severe wound in the head, and the other was carrying a long bag on his shoulder. The third man was armed with a gun. Vetrivel wondered what their intentions were and why they were there. Since they had guns, it was evident that they were aware of the presence of a tiger.

As they approached him, Vetrivel asked, "Who are you? What do you guys want? What happened to him?" Viji stopped him and said, "Let's go inside the house before you ask any more questions. It's not safe outside." "Can't you people see that I am leaving?" "No, you cannot go out. There is a man-eating tiger in the area. It attacked this man while he was riding his motorcycle. Let's go inside and discuss further." Vetrivel stood suspiciously still, but the wounded man looked pitiful and desperately needed help, with his dress torn and covered in heavy bruises. Moreover, Vetrivel noticed that the injured man looked familiar. "Don't worry. We are forest officers. First, let us go into safety, and we will explain everything. Please let us in; you are the only one who can help us."

Vetrivel was reminded of the robbery attempt, but the sight of the wounded man moved him. He opened the gate and rolled his motorcycle in. Arul instructed Viji, "Bring the Jeep. I need medicine. Our basic kit will not help. Careful, Viji." Viji ran out with his gun.

Vetrivel spoke to them: "Just now, a tiger killed and took a man in front of the compound gate and went to the opposite side." Arul was stunned for a minute, gathered himself, and replied, "Yes, we are aware of the situation. We were actually on our way to alert you. It was then that we heard screams and rushed to help. And we found this man lying in the vaikal with his motorcycle on the road and brought him here. We are after it, trying to capture and return it to the reserve." They took the wounded man over the staircase, then through the gate, and settled him on the balcony. While Vetrivel opened the main door, Arul opened his bag, took out the first-aid kit, and started attending to the wounds. Vetrivel returned with a water bottle, sat by Arul's side, and started asking, "What is your name? What is your job in the forest department?" Arul answered him as he cleaned the wounds, "I am Arul. My friend's name is Viji. I am a veterinary doctor and a specialist in preparing tranquillisers and treating animals in reserves. Viji is the sharpshooter. He shoots the animals with the darts I prepare, and then I treat the animals." "Can you treat humans?" was the next question from Vetrivel. Arul replied patiently, "No, I cannot treat serious medical conditions in humans. As we move around forests and wild animals, we are trained to handle and carry medical kits in case of attacks on humans."

Arul finished cleaning the wounds. "These wounds are not deep and serious. The cut in the head needs stitches.

Other than that, everything is fine. He is in shock." Vetrivel asked, "How do you know a tiger is in this place? We had never heard about tigers in this locality. How did a tiger suddenly appear in our locality?" Arul explained, "This tiger was stolen from the reserve near Sathyamangalam, and while it was transported, the vehicle met with an accident, and the tiger escaped. So, my team was asked to follow and find it. The tiger attacked a cattle herd in Ullur and was severely wounded by the cattle it killed. Moreover, the tiger could not find its natural prey, and its wounds made it difficult to hunt the cattle and turned it into a man-eater. Men are easy to kill, and the taste of human flesh also makes it prey on humans." Vetrivel asked, "Are you going to call your people now?" Arul firmly said, "No. Now we will try to locate the tiger and tranquillise it, then call my department people. There are many difficulties in this matter. If we call the department, the media will come. They will spread chaos, and it will disturb everything. Then, the tiger will move to some other place. We should catch it before it widens its territory and establishes itself. It is just the beginning stage of the man-eating habit. It will become very cunning and dangerous if it enters the village and gets used to the men's behaviour. It will be complicated to catch it. So, I request that you cooperate with us. Please keep this between us and do not share it with anyone else."

Arul asked, "Do you live with your family here? Why did you build a house in this lonely place?" Vetrivel started explaining every single detail, from the buying of the land to the tiger killing and carrying his friend. When he finished, Viji drove in the jeep and brought the medical kit. Viji said, "I brought his damaged motorcycle and left it near the fence gate." "Viji, don't worry about it. I will take care of it. This is Vetrivel, the owner of this place. He just saw his friend killed and taken by the tiger. Take your things and follow the trails." To Vetrivel, "Go with him. Show him the spot and the direction in which the tiger went, and come back here." Then to Viji, "Bring him back to the house gate, and then you can go back. I will join you once I have treated him."

Arul took medicine from the Jeep and started treating Mani. He stitched his wounds and administered an injection. By that time, Viji, after knowing the direction the tiger went, brought Vetrivel back to the compound gate. Viji went back, while Vetrivel rejoined Arul and Mani. Vetrivel said, "Your friend is going alone. Can he manage by himself?" Arul replied, "Don't worry. He is a sharpshooter; he can manage.".

Meanwhile, Mani started recovering from the shock and told his part of the story. "Sir, I am Mani. I came looking for my Annan, Maruthu." Mani narrated the events from the day he last saw his brother to how the tiger attacked him on the way to his home. Vetrivel said, "I guessed. I saw his resemblance. But we have not met. I think you can guess what happened to your brother." Mani started crying upon hearing it, and Vetrivel consoled him. Arul was shocked that the tiger had already climbed four victims: the girl, the old man from school, Maruthu, and now Soundar. He thought they should put an end to it, or it would become a disaster.

Arul then helped Mani into the house and rested on the sofa for fifteen minutes. Then he went down, walked to the fence, brought the damaged motorcycle into the compound, parked the Jeep inside the compound, and locked it. His cell phone rang. "Arivalagan, where are you now? Why did you call him? He is trailing the tiger. OK, OK, leave it. He must have put it in silent mode. Call me once you have reached Pallikurichi, and I will pick you up." He slid the phone into his pants pocket. "Idiot … forgot to switch off the phone. I hope at least he put on silent mode." He then went to the terrace of the house and looked around through his binoculars. It was then that he heard two shots fired from Viji's rifle. He hurried down, grabbed his rifle, and ran out. "Is the tiger killed?" eagerly asked Vetrivel. Mani, too, looked at him. "I can't say anything now. Viji needs my help. Lock the doors and don't come out. We will be back soon. Maybe with good news." Arul rushed out of the gate and crossed the mud road.

FOURTEEN

Viji followed the blood trail and the drag left by the poor villager, Soundar. He crossed the mud road and followed the signs. It took him down the mud road and led him into the forest. The forest was mostly open, with trees here and there. Palm Palmyra, Tamarind, Pungai, Peepal, Karu Velam, and Banyan were there but pretty scattered. seemai Karuvi were found everywhere in all sizes. Viji progressed slowly, scanning all the bushes and seemai Karuvi plants. His progress was slow since the forest was new and unlike the one he was familiar with. The blood trail was very thin and in long intervals; tracking alone, without a companion, was difficult. He must look for the trail and also look out for his safety.

Viji was experienced in tracking wounded tigers and leopards. But he always had the company of Arul or some other people. Tracking a normal tiger is less risky compared to a man-eater. Without much experience in tracking a man-eater, Viji felt very uncomfortable. After they entered poaching, Arivalagan used to accompany them. Usually, Arivalagan did the tracking, and they looked out for their safety. Now, Viji was alone, without experience or company.

Viji walked carefully with the gun still in the cover, loaded and ready to fire. His mind urged him to go back and return with Arul and Arivalagan. It's because he doubted his sharp hearing. After the accident, he felt he could not hear the slightest sound. His doubt was confirmed the previous night while sitting on the terrace of the school building. The daylight prevented him from using his thermal imaging equipment, and now he was alone with only his senses and instincts for his safety. The tiger must be busy with his meal, but Viji didn't want to be careless because he is now after an established man-eater whose movements can't be predicted.

The seemai karuvai plants further slowed Viji's progress. These half-grown plants are seen at regular intervals, as though someone had planted them intentionally. The branches shot out from the ground and spread like peacock feathers. So, any animal can hide under it. So, he stopped for a second, carefully scanned the seemai karuvai bushes, and then took a few hurried steps. Again, he stopped, scanned the surroundings, and then moved. He repeated this until he lost the blood trail.

The vegetation started getting thicker, and Viji could no longer see the blood trails. He didn't know in which direction to continue. For a few seconds, he forgot where he stood. Again, he thought that he had made a big mistake. He should have brought Arul with him, or they both should have waited for Arivalagan. Cursing his fate, he decided to walk in the same direction he had so far. Now, another problem stood before him. Thorny Seema Karuvi Kadu stood before him. It was covered with dense karuvai plants. If he had to go through it, he had to either cut them or crawl underneath them. Both ideas were equally dangerous. He didn't want to disturb a hungry man-eating a tiger during its meal.

On the left, next to this land strip, was a *Savuku* plantation. The plantation was very thick and dark. He dropped the idea of going through it. He decided to check how far the seemai karuvai plants were growing on his right side. He walked fifty steps and found clear drag marks under the bushes. The drag marks gave him some confidence. He threw his fear in the air and decided to enter the thorny seemai karuvai Kadu. He pulled out his rifle from the cover, checked if it was loaded, and grabbed his sharp knife. He left the rifle cover and the small bag and started to crawl, with his hands stretched out with the rifle. He was a little happy that he had enough room for his head to look around. The gaps between the plants were wide enough to allow the tiger to drag its meal easily. His progress was very slow; he had to clear the dry twigs of thorns scattered on the ground before he moved, and he crawled zig-zag as he navigated between the thorn plants. When he almost reached the centre of the land, he heard some sounds. He stopped and strained his ears. It was the breaking sound of bones. Indeed, the tiger was having its meal somewhere nearby. The sound came from his right side, and it was behind him. He realised that he had come past it.

He looked at the thick growth of seemai karuvai, and those were young plants with all the branches stretched from the ground to a height of 5 feet, with shining green thorns ranging from half inches to two inches. The thought of going through that thick growth sent chills all over his body. Though the bushes would cover him from an attack, the thorns posed a threat. Moreover, he can't move without making a sound. His legs and back were strained, so he decided to sit for a while and think about his next move. He put his hands with the rifle on the ground, raised his upper body, pulled his legs, and squatted with his knees touching his chest. He took a moment to relax before turning in the direction of the sound. Only then did he realise the sound had stopped, and he couldn't recall when it stopped. He wondered why the sound had stopped. Perhaps the tiger had finished its meal, detected his presence, or moved on to drink water. If the tiger had found him, it would undoubtedly attack him. He looked around fearfully.

The seemai karuvai plants looked safe to him now. The only possible way for the tiger was to crawl under them and attack them. Even then, the tiger won't be able to spring on him. It was well-fed so that it wouldn't risk the thorns. But it could injure him with its claws. When he tried to move the rifle butt to his shoulder, he realised he could not raise his rifle or turn it around. Then, an unexpected thing happened: his cell phone rang. Viji was startled. He hurriedly switched off the phone; his rifle barrel got tangled in the branches in that hurried movement. He slowly pulled the rifle from the plants; he intended to pull it gently, but the thorny branch gave off quickly. The rifle butt came into contact with the ground with a sound, and the branches of the plant shook violently, alerting the tiger if it happened to be nearby and giving away Viji's location to it.

Viji sat with his hands on his head in dismay and fear. He ruined his mission. 'Now what?' If the tiger were nearby, it would check for the source of the sound. Tracing his way out was dangerous, so he decided to stay back and see if the tiger would come to investigate the source of the sound and use that opportunity to shoot it.

He looked around and thought it would be a perfect place to face the tiger. The seemai karuvai plants around him made a rough circle. If he cut the thorny branches of the plant growing in the middle, he could easily turn around and swing his rifle. He can also use the thorns to cover the gaps between the plants. But he must do it fast, so he took out his sharp knife and started cutting it. He also cut a few more branches from nearby plants and added them to the fence. He was happy with the space he had around him. While cutting and fencing, he made a lot of noise, but he was least bothered; anyway, his presence had already been revealed, and now, only his safety mattered.

He checked around his work. The seemai karuvai plants surrounded him with their thorny branches. They had a gap of two feet from the ground before the two plants tangled, and now that gap was covered with the branches cut from the plants. Though he knew this setup wouldn't hold the tiger, it would undoubtedly get him the time he wanted to shoot it. With high hopes and prayers, he started to wait.

Though he looked confident, his inner self was shaking. He was wet thoroughly with sweat, and his palms were mixed with sand and sweat. He could hear the thudding of his heart. That was his first encounter with a man-eater. He checked the cartridges, pressed the safety off, and started to wait, listening to the sounds around him. Nothing happened for around fifteen minutes. There were no animals to warn of the arrival of the tiger. He had mixed thoughts running through his mind, but he was sure that the tiger was around; it was stalking him. The delay in time gave him some confidence in himself.

His strained ears heard a slight movement—the sound of some animal moving through the bushes. He quickly located that the sound was coming from his left. He turned in the direction of the sound after ensuring that a big plant protected his back. He scanned the gaps under the plants but didn't see any animals. Presently, he could hear the sniffing of the animal. Which animal could probably sniff, except a dog? His mind relaxed a little. But what is a dog doing here, he thought? And now a skinny brown stray dog had reached him. It was a poor little bitch, and starvation was written on every single hair of it. It stopped when it reached the enclosure made by him. It gave a short, loud bark and then started whining, wagging its tail. The thorn enclosure stopped it from reaching him. He tried to shuuu it off, but no use; he picked up a stone and threw it at it. The dog lowered its head and started whining.

He started cursing his fate, and by then, the dog's behaviour had changed; it stopped whining and looked silently at Viji and behind him. Its tail went between its legs, and its ears dropped.

When Viji understood the sudden change in the behaviour of the dog, warmness spread all over his body, and he started sweating profusely. He could feel the shivering on his legs. The dog dashed out. Viji knew the tiger was behind him, and it was very close and ready to attack. Now, he should turn around and face it. Suddenly, he lost confidence, and the dog thoroughly distracted him. He was caught unaware. He moved swiftly and turned, pushing himself back until his back touched the thorns. He could see the tiger crawling under the plants. His eyes locked on its face. Was this the tiger they trapped in Sethupalayam? The question flashed in his mind. The face of the tiger was terrible, with several cuts and one eye blackened. It looked terrifying, with its eyes full of anger and hatred. The tiger was stunned by his swift movement. It stopped for a second and crawled fast towards him with a loud growl. The thorns stopped it, and it tried to dislodge the thorns with its claws.

Viji quickly moved the rifle, aimed at the head, and fired. The shot echoed throughout the place. The hurried shot missed the tiger. The tiger swiftly turned around, brushing its body against the thorns, and started to run. Viji shot the second bullet, and it was also a clear miss. The tiger managed to run through the seemai karuvai, known for its sharp thorns. Viji gasped and tried to calm down. He hurriedly emptied the rifle barrel, loaded new cartridges, and started listening for sounds. Then he realised it was the right time to get out of that trap. He started to cut his way out of the seemai karuvai and reached the open ground. He picked up the covers and started walking towards the house. He knew the tiger wouldn't be there in the area; maybe it would move to another area. He cursed himself for what happened. If the tiger moves to another area, tracking it will be difficult. He walked fast, with several thoughts running through his mind. By now, he had almost reached the vaikal before the mud road. If he crossed that road, he would reach the safety of the house. Then he heard the sharp alarm cry of the Karung Kurangu. The sound came from the opposite direction. Viji immediately stopped. Viji knew the call. It was a signal from Arul to warn that their target was nearby.

He immediately scanned the trees opposite him. Then, in the bushes, he located Arul's rifle barrel. Chillness ran through his body. Tiger had been following him. He was shocked; he walked further to the bush, then swiftly stepped away from Arul's line of fire. He swiftly turned around and lay on his stomach, uncovered his rifle, removed the safety, and scanned the bushes. Viji scanned the bushes he came through, but there was no movement. "Look slightly to your right; the Aavaarai bushes that are 30 feet away," Arul said in a low voice. Viji turned to the bushes. It was an avaram shrub commonly found with yellow flowers. He scanned every leaf and finally located a black object. Viji recognised the black object: the hair of the tiger's ears. Suddenly, it disappeared, as though it sensed him watching it. A few minutes passed by, and a bush behind it moved slightly. Viji relaxed, "Finally, it gave up," he said to himself, but he lay still. Arul walked out and called, "Viji, what happened to you? Have you lost your senses after the accident?" Viji thoughtfully replied, "I thought the tiger ran away. It took the two shots from point-blank range. I thought it might have scared it off. But this one is different." "Viji, I am surprised you missed the tiger in point-blank range. Don't forget, we are dealing with a man-eater. Let us go. You badly need a rest. Arivalagan will be here. We should pick him up from Palikurichi," said Arul. They walked slowly to the house, looking around and scanning all the sides. After lunch, Arul and Viji took some rest on the balcony.

Viji narrated the events to Arul. Viji said, "The tiger is disfigured and beyond recognition. It has lost its hair, a lot of cuts, and half-healed wounds on its face. I think it lost its left eye." Then they slept. By 5.30 p.m., Arivalagan called them from Palikurichi. Arul picked him up and explained the situation on the drive back.

FIFTEEN

On reaching the house, Arivalagan wasted no time and instructed Arul to sketch a rough map of the village and its surroundings. Vetrivel provided them with the necessary details, and together, they marked the spots of kills and the spot where Viji had encountered the tiger. The areas of activity of the tiger ranged from the savukku plantation to the house, along the mud road, and even across the main road towards the school and the road leading to Melaiyur. "We still have an hour of daylight left. Tonight, we will watch from the three most frequented locations: the savukku plantation, the tree near the mud road where the girl was killed, and the school building."

"Do you think the tiger will kill another human tonight? It just had a meal in the afternoon," asked Viji doubtfully. Arul had the same doubt but was hesitant to ask. Arivalagan stared at Viji and replied, "It is a man-eater; it can't be predicted. So, let us be prepared."

"Oh! Ok, then, I will sit over the savukku trees if you make a perfect Paran. I know the place well," confidently stated Viji. "Good. Arul will sit on the terrace of the school building. I will take the tree." Arul asked, "What about your weapon?" "I don't have any. How can I bring the rifle on the bus?" Arul responded, "No problem; you take my rifle, and I will use my tranquiliser." Moreover, the school is very close to the village. If I had to shoot, the whole village would hear it. First, let us put up Viji's paran, and then we can take up our places," said Arul. "Do you have a ladder?" asked Arivalagan. Vetrivel pointed the stairs to the terrace and said, "There are two ladders." Arivalagan, without wasting time, climbed the terrace and quickly grabbed the aluminium ladder while Arul and Viji unloaded the hunting tree stand from the jeep and unfolded it. Arivalagan asked, "Do you think you can tie these stands to Savukku trees? These trees are not big enough to hold the stand. We can't use our string cots, too. Do you have bamboo and wooden planks?". Arivalagan pointed to the terrace. "There are bamboo and Savuku poles, wooden planks, and ropes used for centring works, covered in tarpaulins." All three reached the terrace and climbed down with the necessary things. The three walked out towards the Savukku thoppu. Arivalagan asked, "Do they have cell phones?" "No," replied Arul. "What if they go out?" "Do you think they will go out after watching all the happenings? Don't worry about them."

Arivalagan walked into the Savukku thoppu, looking for the right spot, while Arul and Viji took guard. "Look, these trees won't hold the tree stand." He pointed to the ground and said, "The dry leaves on the ground make a soft bed. But it will tell you the approach of the tiger." He selected four trees that stood on the edge of the thoppu, facing the Semmai karuvai Kadu.

The four trees were stout and strong, high enough to construct the paran, and the needle-like leaves gave a perfect natural cover. Arivalagan used the ladder to cut the side branches. He used four sturdy five feet bamboo to connect the four trees. The bamboos they brought were accurate since the gap between the trees was precisely one-and-a-half metres. Then another problem showed up: the wooden planks they had were only four feet. Arivalagan kept the wooden planks diagonally and tied them. Now, Viji was restricted to sitting in one corner with his back to one tree. He used two more bamboos above the paran for hand grip to prevent Viji from falling from the paran and used all the excess ropes to tie it crisscross like a net, which the wooden planks could not cover. It would prevent Viji from hanging his legs and falling off the platform.

Finally, the paran was ready, and the very look of it made them uncomfortable and insecure, but they had no time to spare. Viji climbed up the ladder and occupied the paran. He felt a little satisfied that the structure was beyond his expectations. It was not as weak as it looked from the ground. Arivalagan handed over the equipment and rifle, and both walked off with the ladder. They again climbed the road, dropped the aluminium ladder inside the gate, and walked towards the main road. They walked on the mud road. Arivalagan got down and walked towards the tree. Arul waited until Arivalagan reached the tree, then he walked towards the main road and reached the school. He turned left on the Melaiyur road, walked down the odai, and entered the school. He reached the school building, climbed it, and settled on the terrace.

As darkness set in, questions flooded the mind of Arul. Why was the tiger's movement confined to this village and forest? Even after being shot at point-blank range, why did it still try to attack Viji? And why hadn't it ventured into the village or attacked anyone on the main road? Every question plunged him deeper into the darkness. He knew only an experienced man-eater hunter could answer. Arul made up his mind that he would wait until the next day. Then he would ask Vetrivel and Mani to complain to the police and disappear from the scene.

Crickets started chirping, and though the area was dry, there were a lot of mosquitoes biting him in turns. He took out the mosquito repellent and applied it. There were a few two-wheelers on the road, mostly lonely riders. Arul looked at them with fear. The first thing that occurred to him was, what if the tiger attacked one of the riders? He prayed that no such mishaps would happen. He took out his thermal image binoculars and started scanning the area in front of the school and the roads. He could not catch any images of life or any movement. He also realised that the vaikal on the other side of the road and the twenty-foot-long bridge standing over the odai on the Melaiyur road had a great cover, and the compound wall on that side also obstructed his view. He felt that spot could be a good hide for the tiger to attack the riders. He felt he should have taken the kitchen building closer to the bridge instead of the classroom block.

He started scanning along the roads and then scanning the dark spots under the bridge. He repeated this pattern until his thermal imager caught a small red object on the edge between the bridge and the vaikal. It stood still for some time and gradually grew in size, and the head of the tiger appeared. Arul quickly dropped the thermal binoculars, took the dart rifle, and looked through the thermal scope. The spot was clear, and the tiger was gone. His prediction was about to come true; the tiger was planning to attack a two-wheeler rider. Hurriedly, he started to search again. After around fifteen minutes, the head appeared on the other side of the bridge, near the school. Now, Arul could see the back of its head. He couldn't fire the dart at the head, but the shoulders or neck would be a perfect spot to fire a dart, so he started to wait.

To make the situation worse, a motorcycle approached the bridge. Arul got tensed and didn't know what to do if he turned towards Melaiyur. He decided to fire the dart to distract the tiger from attacking the rider. As anticipated, the man took the bridge. Arul took position and prepared to fire when he saw its shoulder or neck. The two-wheeler came near the tiger, and the light fell partially on its head, but the man did not notice the tiger. He crossed it and rode safely. Arul got a little relieved. When he looked through the scope, the tiger was gone. He was worried the tiger was chasing the man, so he took the binoculars and scanned the road. And he felt relieved to see that the road was clear. He could see the tail lamp of the two-wheeler speeding steadily towards the village.

He guessed that the tiger was still stalking there. Again, he scanned the area near the bridge. After some five minutes, the head appeared on the opposite side. Now, he understood that the tiger was using the cover of the bridge, traversing under it, to switch its place. Tigers always need the element of surprise to hunt their prey. Its previous location was revealed when the man turned around the corner. The light from the motorcycle could have easily spotted it. So, it changed sides. Now, the head appeared over the edge of the road, close to the side wall of the bridge, waiting for another rider. Suddenly, Arul was reminded of his high-beam torch light. He took it out and pointed at the area the tiger was stalking, looked around for a second, and switched it on. The light fell straight on the face of the tiger. It was stunned and looked at the light source. With a loud snarl, it disappeared. Arul started to scan around. The tiger just vanished. He looked down at the ground and the side of the building he was sitting on. He thought he had frightened the tiger, and it disappeared.

He thought, what if the tiger entered the village and took a person? He didn't know what would happen next. No other choice but to wait. Patience was always rewarded in the jungle. So, he decided to continue his efforts. Tired off a bit, he lay on the terrace and relaxed, then a thought occurred: what if the tiger comes to inspect the source of light? But he knew the building was too high for the tiger to climb. After dozing off for nearly an hour, he was abruptly awakened by a sound that sounded like something landing on the logs, followed by logs rolling down from a pile. The sound came near the gate of the school. He lay still, then crept to the edge and looked towards the gate. There were wooden logs piled up near the second abandoned kitchen to use as firewood. On the previous days, it was not there. He had not seen the piled firewood since he entered the school through the odai. Chillness ran through his body. The kitchen's roof was sloppy. The tiger could have easily jumped on the pile of wood from the compound, from there to the kitchen roof, then onto the roof of the building near the gate, and then could jump to the building he was on. He felt foolish and started thinking about his next move. He was equipped with a dart rifle. Even if he managed to shoot the tiger, it would kill him before the drug immobilised it. He had no other option but to escape the spot.

He turned and laid on his belly and then started to crawl towards the left side of the building, slowly sliding to the sun shade, climbed down and landed on the ground. He wanted a hideout. He was reminded that the metal door of the toilets was not locked. But he had to jump over the wall and enter the toilet block. He could clearly hear a dull thump when he was about to jump over the wall. The tiger had jumped into his building. He slowly climbed over the wall, landed on the floor, opened the door, entered, latched it from inside, and pressed his back against the wall. He was thoroughly shaken. He left behind all his equipment in a hurry to escape. He stood in the corner, sweating and trembling. After a few minutes, he could feel the weight of the tiger fall above him. The tiger walked around that narrow roof and then jumped behind the toilet.

Arul felt relieved and sat on the floor. His legs shivered, and his sweat dripped on the floor. He decided to wait there until the sun. But he heard the warning call from Arivalagan. Arivalagan had seen the tiger moving towards Viji and was warning him. He jumped out of the toilet, climbed up the terrace, and gave a full-throated reply call. Again, Arivalagan signalled that the tiger had crossed him. Arul immediately packed his things, climbed down the building, and walked towards the tree.

SIXTEEN

Viji settled himself on the paran after Arul and Arivalagan left him. He sat in one corner, with his back to the way they came in and facing the savuku thoopu and karuvai kadu. From his vantage point, he could see the area where he had previously seen action earlier that day. The circle he had made with thorns during his previous encounter was visible, and he also noticed a clearing in the centre where logs were scattered and there were no seemai karuvai plants. Viji thought that could be the perfect hiding spot for the tiger and decided to check it out tomorrow.

Viji secured the bag to a nearby tree using the rope he had brought with him for the purpose. He checked his thermal binoculars and kept them by his side. He took out his dart rifle, fixed the thermal scope, and loaded the dart prepared by Arul. Then, he took out the .12 double-barrel bore gun to ensure that the slug head cartridges were loaded in it. He clamped the rifle torch, threw the safety catch open, and kept it ready by his side. He took out his cell phone and switched it off. He wanted to avoid repeating the mistake and started his night-long wait for the man-eater.

A normal tiger won't return to the spot where it got shot and narrowly escaped. But this tiger was not a normal one. As the time passed and the light faded away, he reached the bag, took out a plastic box, opened it, and ate some biscuits. He drank some water; some hot tea would have been better, but they had no time for the luxury of it.

Soon, the place was dark, and the place where he sat went dark earlier than the other places. The place was very cold, and he looked in the bag for something to cover him. Several thoughts ran through his mind. What would happen if the tiger shifted its place or entered the village while they were sitting here all night? In villages, most people preferred to sleep in the open. When the tiger learned it, it would be a disaster. What should be the next move when they dart or shoot the tiger? Why is the tiger clinging to this area? The tiredness overtook him, and he dozed off.

Meanwhile, Arivalagan's place on the tree was uncomfortable, but he was used to such situations. The *pungai* tree started branching at a height of 10 feet, and then there were several big branches, and the tree was covered with new green leaves.

The *pungai* tree usually sheds leaves in the last days of February, and there will be only the branches left at the beginning of March. Then, the new, greener leaves would appear. It was the final days of April, so the tree was full of new green leaves.

Arivalagan took out the rope, tied the bag and rifle, and then looked at the high branches. Though those branches were strong, they were not safe to sit on. They were only four inches, and he couldn't sit on them throughout the night. So, he chose a long, 2-inch-thick branch, took out his small sickle, cut it into three 2-foot-long logs, and then tied them to the branch with the rope he had brought. Now he had the perfect seat to sit in for the night—not comfortable but safe. He untied the bag and rifle and tied them near his seat. He took out the biscuits from the cloth and started munching them. He took out his cell phone and checked the time. It was 6.45; he switched it off and threw it in the bag. Unlike Arul and Viji, he didn't have thermal binoculars because he didn't know how to use them. He always relied on his senses.

After refreshing himself with biscuits and water, he tied his bag to the tree. He checked the rifle and cartridges, clamped the torch, and kept it ready to fire. The night passed smoothly; if it were a forest, there would be animals and birds to warn him of the presence of a predator; here, he missed those animals that would warn him. He had to rely on his senses.

There was minimal traffic on the road. Then and there, a two-wheeler appeared. He could see the headlights of the two-wheelers on the main road as dots from his position. He thought for a while that he should have taken a place near the road. If the tiger killed a two-wheeler rider, they would be ruined. He stared at the lights as they passed towards the Melaiyur Road, or Karuppukudi. Time passed, and slowly, he could see the trees around him. The moonlight lit the area. When a two-wheeler appeared on the road, his eyes followed them to see if they were disturbed by the tiger. His eyes would follow the tail lamps until they disappeared.

Then he noticed a high-beam torch flashing from the roof of the school building. It took a minute for Arivalagan to realise it was Arul. Certainly, he must have spotted the tiger. He could see the light moving in all directions along the building, and then it switched off. It was clear that Arul had spotted the tiger but missed it. Now, the question of Arul's safety flashed through his mind. He was worried that if the tiger climbed the building, it would kill Arul. He felt sorry for taking his rifle. The dart would take time to pacify the tiger; by then, the tiger would have easily killed him. He started to wait with mixed thoughts, glancing at the school building.

Almost an hour passed, and Arivalagan sensed a slight movement in the land beyond the mud road. Though he could see only the shadow, he knew it was the tiger. The next thought that ran through his mind was to check if it carried any humans, especially Arul. In the next few steps, the tiger came into full view. It walked slowly, looking in all directions. It was going towards the house. It should either go to Viji and get shot or try its luck at the house. He gave a full-throated warning call to Viji. Only Arul replied to it after a few minutes. Through another call, he signalled to Arul that the tiger had crossed him. Viji must have gotten his warning, he thought. Soon, he saw Arul running towards him. He gathered his bag and rifle, tied them to the rope, and lowered them to the ground. He then slowly climbed down and joined Arul. Both of them walked towards Viji.

Viji was sleeping peacefully without being disturbed by the alarm call from Arivalagan. But abruptly, he woke up; his senses warned him of danger. It was pitch-black around him. He sat still, and his eyes got used to the darkness in a few minutes. The place was very silent; even the crickets went silent, and there was the occasional sound of a two-wheeler on the road. He took out his thermal binoculars and started scanning around. Just then, there was a sudden, violent shake on the paran. The binoculars fell on his lap, and he hurriedly grasped them. The violent shake continued, and now with a deep growl. He turned around and saw the tiger trying to climb on the paran. And it chose the tree to which he was leaning with his back. With one bounce, it reached around 12 feet easily. It badly wanted to claim the paran or dislodge Viji. Fortunately, the paran was well placed above 15 feet. Viji hung the binoculars around his neck and held on to the side supporting poles.

Viji slowly turned around, stood on all fours, and faced the tiger. He saw the tiger staring at him with a thunderous growl. Viji started to sweat, and his hold on the poles was slippery. Hurriedly, he rubbed his palms against his shirt. In the meantime, Arul and Arivalagan reached the house. They walked down the road and proceeded towards Viji's location. After a few minutes of walking, they heard the growling sound of the tiger and understood Viji's critical position. Both stalked the distance carefully, halted, and took a secure position. Both closed on the scene carefully to bring the dart rifle into close range. Arul handed the thermal binoculars to Arivalagan and signalled him to look out, and he took a position with his dart gun.

The tiger got furious after seeing Viji's face. When Viji stretched out his hands to grab the rifle, the tiger made one unexpected giant leap. This time, it almost touched the paran and tried climbing. The impact was strong, and Viji lost his hold and was thrown back. He fell on one of the gaps of the crisscrossed rope, and the ropes were not tight; his bottom got stuck in the gap. He could not get up and climb back up the paran, and slowly, the rope gave away. Viji was slipping through the gap, folded like the alphabet V. The tiger fell to the ground on its back, and Viji slipped through the gap and landed on the ground close to the tiger. The impact on the ground was heavy, and Viji started to cry loudly.

The tiger got back on its feet, saw Viji wailing, and ran towards him. Viji saw the tiger coming towards him. He wanted to stand up but couldn't. With all his strength, he started kicking frantically in the air. His legs kicked the face of the tiger. The tiger mauled his right leg with its claws. The muscle was torn and hanging loose like a ribbon. It bit him in the left thigh and lifted him. Viji couldn't move his legs and started hitting the tiger, but to no avail. His hands caught the ears of the tiger, and with a sharp cry, he twisted its ears with his full strength. The tiger was annoyed. It dropped him and went for his throat, but he held his forearms and turned sideward. The tiger bit him on the shoulder and tried to lift him; he wailed in pain. But he kept his fighting spirit alive.

It took a minute for Arul and Arivalagan to realise the happenings. Arivalagan hesitated to use the gun, for it would miss and might wound Viji. So they started running towards him, shouting in full throat. Arivalagan raised the rifle above his head and almost fired to distract the tiger. It was then that another unexpected thing happened. The rifle of Viji slipped through the gap left in the paran, and the rifle butt came into violent contact with the ground and fired with a thunderous sound. The slug veered above the heads of Arul and Arivalagan. Luckily, it missed them, or else it would have been fatal to one of them.

The tiger dropped Viji and rushed out of the scene towards the house. With one bounce, it dashed through the bushes, took the road, and went behind the house. Viji lay on the ground, bleeding profusely from all the holes and cuts made by the tiger. Arul and Arivalagan reached him and found him wailing in the pool of blood and sweat running all over his body. Arul grabbed the rifle, switched on the light, and examined the wounds. Arivalagan picked up Viji's rifle and switched on the light. The mauled leg was bleeding, the muscles were hanging loosely, and the wounds on the shoulder and thigh were deep. Arul and Arivalagan took out the medical kits from the bag and started attending to the wounds. Arul tied the bandages to the mauled leg and tried to stop the bleeding. Arul administered two injections—antibiotics and painkillers—to Viji. After a few minutes, the bleeding was stopped. Arul and Arivalagan relaxed a bit. Arul had seen worse. Out of experience and habit, he always carried a complete medical kit in his bags. Viji also had a basic kit in his bag.

Arivalagan climbed the Savuku tree, reached the paran, tied the bag to the rope, and lowered it. Then he dismantled the paran and climbed down. "Let us take him to the house and then come back to collect the bags," said Arul. "Sure, let me pack them and keep them ready before we go. And it will give Viji some time to relax." Arivalagan started packing the bags, and he collected all the blood-stained bandages and cotton and put them in a cover. Arul picked up Viji's rifle and said, "Your rifle saved your life but almost took ours.".

Arivalagan, when he was about to pick up the bags and keep them aside, stood still, straining his ears, and grabbed the hands of Arul. He stared at Arul and Viji. Both knew what he meant. He had sensed the danger. They also knew the habits of the tiger. Viji took the binoculars hanging from his neck and scanned the area. He saw the hidden body of the tiger that was stalking them. Now, its head was hidden behind one of the Savukku trees. Arul took his dart rifle, raised it to his shoulder, and looked through the thermal scope. The tiger was just 50 feet away. He was surprised by the boldness of it. It was the second time it got the heavy impact of the rifle at close range. But still, it was bold enough to stalk them. He thought maybe the tiger was getting used to the sound. Next time, it will not run away but attack at the sound of the rifle. Still, it was waiting behind the tree. They switched off the lights and sat still.

Arul got an idea; Arivalagan and Viji were on both sides. If they flashed their torches at the tiger, the light would blind it, and it would be stunned for a few seconds. Then Arul would fire the dart. He grabbed their rifle barrel and turned it towards the tiger. Through experience, both Viji and Arivalagan understood his plan. Viji held up his rifle with his shaky hands. Arivalagan and Viji got ready with their fingers on the switch. All three were shaking inside, but as a team, they had confidence. Arul saw through the scope, and now the tiger moved; first, the head and then the shoulder came into view. The left shoulder of the tiger came in position with Arul's rifle; without a move, he could fire the dart. Arul nudged Arivalagan, who was standing to his left. He switched on the torch first, and Viji followed him. The tiger was stunned by the light and hesitated for a few seconds. It was enough for Arul; he fired the dart. The tiger let out a growl and dashed out. They hurriedly picked up Viji, turned around, walked out of the Savukku thoppu, and walked towards the house.

Arul checked the time; it was almost midnight. "It was a perfect hit. We will check around after one hour. First, let us attend to Viji's wound. Or else he will develop an infection." They hurried through the fence gate, and Vetrivel waited till they reached the compound gate, climbed downstairs, and opened it for them. "What happened?" nervously asked Vetrivel. "The tiger attacked and wounded him. But still, we had tranquilised it. First let us clean his wounds, and then we shall track and secure the tiger." Arul answered him as they walked through the gate. Then they entered the house; Vetrivel and Mani helped Arul take Viji upstairs.

They deposited him on the floor of the hall. Arul and Arivalagan went back to bring the bag and equipment. When they came back, Viji had dozed off. Arul started to remove the bandage and started to clean off the wounds. He made several stitches on the mauled leg. Once the wounds were done, everyone lay on the floor exhausted, the lights were switched off, and the doors locked. No one slept; everyone had deep thoughts running through their minds. After some twenty minutes, they heard honking sounds outside. Vetrivel rushed out, opened the door, and saw three motorcycles standing near the compound gate. All of them joined him. They all walked down the stairs. Arul signalled Arivalagan and Mani to go with him. "Who are they? What are they here for?" asked Arul. Vetrivel replied, "I don't know. It must be the villagers. Maybe they came looking for my friend Soundar". "Remember what I told you and speak carefully. If they ask about us, Tell them we were here for plantation work, Arul warned Arivalagan. "The tiger is sedated, but keep your sickle ready." Arivalagan grabbed his sickle. He understood what Arul really meant.

The three walked in silence towards the gate. Vetrivel was a little happy to see his friends. It was Sanjai and his friends. Sanjai had his lands at the edge of the village. Almost one-and-a-half kilometres from the house. But he wondered what brought them here. Sanjai asked, "What was that blasting sound? I thought it came from here. Also, I saw torch lights in the Savukku thoppu. We thought there could be some problems. I just came to check if everything was fine. Is there any problem?" "No, the sound came from the road. It must be the truck tyre. These people came here for plantation work. They came out to answer the call of nature and saw a wild rabbit and tried to catch it." "Oh, we were reminded of the previous incident in your home. So, we came to check on you. said Sanjai. "If there is any problem, I will let you know." Vetrivel was happy that they didn't ask anything about Soundar. They were convinced for now, but they were not convinced about the gun sound.

Meanwhile, Arul cleaned the floor, checked the wounds on Viji, and sedated him. Then they moved him to the room on the first floor. Arul and Arivalagan lay down on the bed for a nap. Arul set a wake-up alarm after 2:30 a.m. The two-hour gap would allow the drugs to take effect on the tiger and also give some time for Vetrivel's friends to reach their homes and settle down. Moreover, they themselves badly needed a nap.

SEVENTEEN

At around 2:30 a.m., Arul and Arivalagan gathered their night equipment and a good supply of ropes. Then, they approached Vetrivel and asked him to join them. Vetrivel expressed shock and asked, "Are you serious? Should I go with you?" Arul assured him, "Yes, don't worry. It's safe. Do you think we would risk your life? The tiger is tranquilised, or else we won't take you with us. You are the only one who knows the area." They started to walk out of the house. Arul and Arivalagan walked in front, and Vetrivel walked behind them. When they tried to level him, he purposely fell behind them. Then, Arul advised, "Tigers usually take the one in the last. Stay in line with us."

The three walked out of the compound, locking behind them. Arivalagan handed a torch to Vetrivel and explained his plan: "First, we will go to the Savukku thoppu. From there, we will follow any trail we find." To Vetrivel, he said, "Sir, always stay in the middle of us. And speak only when you are spoken to. If you want to say something, just touch us." Both switched on the hunting torches attached to their foreheads. They crossed the road and walked towards the Savuku Thoppu and karuvai Kadu.

After a fifteen-minute walk, they reached the spot where Viji was attacked. The place was stinking with the remains of Soundar. Arivalagan said, "Arul, you stay here with sir. I will check the place; Viji told us yesterday." Arivalagan started to make his way, cutting through the seemai karuvai plants to reach the spot. Arul and Vetrivel walked out of the savukku thoppu and sat on the open ground. From there, they could see Arivalagan with a torchlight and hear the sound of cutting the plants.

As they guessed, that place was the retreat of the tiger, and it ate its kill there. The place was stinking from the remains of Soundar. There were a few splinters of bones, the left out inner parts of Soundar, and a few torn clothes. He had seen tigers leave the heads, legs, and hands of their victims without eating. He had also heard that if the tiger was not disturbed and the hunt was scarce, they would eat the head, hands, and legs too. Now, he is witnessing the second condition. There were no heads or legs. After Viji left, the tiger must have had its meals. He collected the old lungi with blood stains. He also saw a blue-coloured torn pant cloth. He collected them and walked back to Arivalagan and Arul.

"These are the only remains of Soundar. All the parts were eaten." Arivalagan gave the cloth bits to Arul, pointed to the pant cloth, and continued, "I think the tiger had another victim. The pant cloth looks very old. We should inquire who else is missing." Then, the three walked to the spot where the tiger was darted. Arul and Arivalagan carefully examined the ground. But the ground in the Savukku thoppu was covered with the dried leaves of Savukku, so they could not see any. But the experienced eyes of Arivalagan could see the impression on the dried leaves, for the leaves were cupped in because of the tiger's weight.

This faint track was found until the Savukku thoppu. It led them towards the road and the Semmai karuvai Kadu near it. Arul again checked the surroundings with the thermal binoculars to ensure that there was no thermal image of an animal. They further entered the karuvai kadu. From there, they could see the top of the house in the distance. Arivalagan started cutting branches of seemai karuvai to make a pass-through. After half an hour's walk, they reached a small open field and the mud road, the place where the tiger killed Maruthu. They carefully scanned the area and found the cycle and blood-stained vesti. While Arul and Viji were busy checking the cycle, Arivalagan found the old button phone of Marthu, and hurriedly, he slid it in his pocket. He then rolled all the clothes in the vesti as a bundle and clipped them onto the cycle carrier. Then he rolled the cycle to the gate, left it there, and joined the team.

Arul said, "There are no hiding places behind the house. Yesterday, I checked from the terrace. So, we better take this mud road and see if there are any places for the tiger to hide." Vetrivel said, "This mud road goes to a limestone mine, and they laid this mud road. They were mining limestone and transporting it to the factory near Samayapuram, Trichy. Now they closed it since the transport cost of limestone is high." Arul felt that the mine could be an ideal hiding spot for the tiger, so they walked straight to the mines. They stopped several feet before the gate. The mud road ended near the mines, at the gate, and then the road continued as a footpath. Arul asked Vetrivel, "Is there any other way to sneak in?" Vetrivel pointed to the left. Arul scanned the area through the thermal binoculars and proceeded in that direction. They stepped down the road, entered the bushy part, and negotiated through it. After a five-minute walk, they reached the side of the mines. They could see the fence. Vetrivel pointed at the fence, and they walked towards it. Vetrivel showed them the hole, made by the local boys, to sneak in and take a bath. They got through it. Arul and Arivalagan were surprised to see the thick vegetation inside the mines. They could see a lot of pungai trees. The first building they encountered was the overhead water tank.

The water tank stood on four cement concrete pillars. It had a metal ladder to climb the tank and clean it. Arul pointed the ladder to Vetrivel. Vetrivel climbed it up, and Arul followed him. Arivalagan stayed down for a while, and then he, too, joined them. Arul scanned the place with binoculars, first in thermal mode and then in night vision mode. To the left of the water tank, the land was flat for around five hundred metres, and the mining area started. The land fell deep, and the ground was flooded and looked like a big lake with trees around it. The office and quarters were located to the right of the water tank, and then there was a shed near the gate.

Arul signalled for Vetrivel to stay in the tank. Arul and Arivalagan climbed down and walked towards the mining area with the help of night vision. They stopped over the edge. Arul quickly switched to thermal mode, assessed the surroundings, and then switched back to night vision. He concluded that it was an extremely dangerous location to descend into and decided that the only safe approach was to take the truck road, which had an entrance near the office.

Arul and Arivalagan looked at each other. Arivalagan pointed to the quarters. They walked towards it. They checked for an entry other than the main gate. But there was no point of entry. So, they moved to the garage and spotted an open window. The room used as the garage was previously used as an office room, and it had a provision for window AC. Now, the window AC was removed, and a door was installed. But the door was broken and hung loosely. Arul pointed to the dark stains on the wall and the window. Then, they cautiously approached the window and scanned the inside in thermal and night vision modes. There was no sign of the tiger. The room smelled of grease and tyres. Arivalagan went through the window while Arul stood outside. Arivalagan switched on his hunting torch, checked the room for a few minutes, and then came out.

They walked towards the water tank and signalled for Vetrivel to come down. Then, the three traced their way out in silence after reaching the spot beyond the mud road. Arivalagan said, "Another victim must be the watchman of the mines. The blue pant cloth is the uniform. I saw a torn old pant in the room. The tiger must have killed him in the room and then taken him to the spot. There was a blood trail from that place to the window." "You are correct; a few days before he went missing, Maruthu told me about the murder of a watchman in the mines," said Vetrivel. Arivalagan looked at the watch and said, "It is almost four. We better go back. Let us leave things to happen and wait for the next chance."

Then, they heard the engine sound of a pickup truck in the distance. "Where does that sound come from?" asked Arul. Vetrivel replied, "There is a *meen kuttai* on the other side of the village. We should continue on the footpath beyond the mud road." replied Vetrivel, and he started walking towards it. Arul and Arivalagan followed him. They traced back the way they came, reached the footpath near the mines, and walked towards it. After a swift walk of fifteen minutes, they reached the meen kuttai. Arul looked at his watch. It was 4:30, and the people were busy catching the fish, weighing them, and filling them in the crate. Then, the crates were loaded into the pickups and sent to the shops.

Arul signalled them to turn around. They walked silently towards the house. On reaching the gate, Arivalagan rolled the bicycle to the parking area under the house and parked it near the Jeep. Arul went to Viji and checked on him. Everyone lay down on the available sofa and bed and soon fell asleep. Vetrivel felt relieved and happy that he reached home alive. Vetrivel's mind began to doubt the behaviour of Arul and his friends. He was worried that they were postponing the decision to inform the police or the forest department. But he was very clear in his idea of letting things happen.

EIGHTEEN

At 6:30 a.m., Mani woke up and saw everyone sleeping peacefully. He began walking around. He felt energetic and decided to go outside the compound to answer nature's call while others were fast asleep. He came out, crossed the mud road, remembered Viji's encounter in the area, scanned the area carefully, sat by a spot near seemai karuvai bushes, and finished his work. Then he went inside the house, brought a bucket, and went to the ground floor. When he crossed the Jeep and went near the tap, he saw the cycle of his brother. For an instant, he thought his brother was back. But the torn, blood-stained clothes clipped to the carrier of the cycle reminded him of reality. He sat and wept for his brother, consoled himself, bathed in the tap, and washed his shirt and pants. Leaning on the Jeep, he thought about his brother and his ill fate while his dress dried. He decided to do all the last rituals, though he didn't get any part of his brother. He felt starving. The last meal he had was breakfast the previous morning. Everyone in the house had only biscuits for dinner the previous night, so he decided to prepare some breakfast.

He put on his clothes and started climbing the stairs. When he reached the gate and locked it behind him, he saw some movement in the far-distant corner of the field, in the

Seema karuvai bushes. He stopped for a moment and looked at the place. But he didn't see anything. He then walked to the kitchen, checked the groceries, and prepared *rava upma* and coconut chutney. He ate his part and waited for others to wake up.

Around ten, everyone woke up, refreshed themselves, ate breakfast happily, and then sat down to decide that day's work. Arul made the final decision: "I am sure that the tiger has found a safe place, and it won't be out till the tranquilliser loses its effect, and that would be late afternoon or dusk. So, I will leave Arivalagan with you to help Viji, and I will go to Thanjavur to buy the medicines needed for Viji and return in the afternoon. Then we will decide on the next plan." He also firmly said, "We will try our hands today. If we fail, we inform the department, call in all available forces, and the tiger will be either trapped or killed." To Vetrivel and Mani: "Don't do anything stupid, and please wait till tomorrow morning. Hope you both understand and help us."

Arul took his Jeep and drove away. Arivalagan, after nursing Viji, said, "I will go around looking for traces of the tiger. If the tiger had moved to another location, it would have been very dangerous. So, I will move around the nearby villages and check for news. I also want to explore the places around us. Will you take care of Viji?" Vetrivel replied, "It's okay for us. But we have to call our family. Otherwise, they will be worried." Arivalagan gave his phone to Vetrivel and said, "Yes, I almost forgot about it in the happenings. Don't tell them anything. Just tell them you have work and will return in the morning."

Vetrivel made the first call. "Okay, okay... I understand... My phone fell and broke... This phone is from a friend of

Maruthu... No, Maruthu is not here... We couldn't find him. But I managed to find his brother... We are looking for his whereabouts...I will come in the morning... Don't worry... okay, if you need to call...call this number."

Mani called his wife. "This is my friend's number. My phone fell and was damaged. No, brother is not here. The owner is here, and we are looking for him. We will try today, complain to the police tomorrow, and then return... Don't worry... We don't know where he went... Okay, if anything is urgent, call me at this number." Arivalagan took Vetrivel's motorcycle and rode out. Before leaving, he warned them not to leave the house.

Vetrivel and Mani didn't know what to do. Both stood on the balcony near the gate. Mani told Vetrivel about his encounter with the tiger. He felt sorry that he was also a reason for the tiger becoming a man-eater. He requested that Vetrivel not disclose it to Arul and Arivalagan. Vetrivel said, "These guys and their activities look suspicious to me. We should inform someone. If I could get a phone, I could inform a friend in the police department and ask for his help." Mani said, "Let us search their stuff. We can find something useful." They went to the room and sat by Viji. Viji was sleeping soundly after the medication.

Vetrivel sat by Viji's side while Mani searched the bags of Arul and his team. He found the cell phone of Maruthu hidden under the clothes in Arivalagan's bag. Mani showed it to Vetrivel and then walked out of the room. Vetrivel sat for some time, followed him, and joined him. Mani said, "Your suspicion about them is correct. These people should not be trusted. Why should they hide my brother's phone?"

"Does the phone have any battery left?" asked Vetrivel. "No. The charger will be in the shed. I will fetch it. We should do that before they come." Vetrivel went into his room, brought the spare key, handed it to Mani, and said, "I will go with you." Both walked out of the house. Mani stopped Vetrivel and said, "What if Viji woke up? He would doubt us. You better stay here, sir." Mani sounded correct.

Vetrivel stood watching while Mani ran towards the shed. He unlocked the door and locked it behind him. Vetrivel stood there restlessly. He felt the time was dragging. Mani opened the door after ten minutes. He hurried back and gave the cell phone and charger to Vetrivel. "It's working. I charged it in the shed." "Give it to me. I will call a friend in the police department and inform him of the situation." Vetrivel climbed downstairs, stood on the last stair, and made a call.

Meanwhile, Mani went back to Viji to check on him. When he returned, Vetrivel had finished the call and was waiting for him. Vetrivel whispered to Mani, "My friend told me to call him when they were back. He also told me to lock them in the house, if possible." "What about the tiger? Have you told them?" asked Mani. "Yes, I told him. He will inform the Forest Department. We will end this story tonight," replied Vetrivel firmly. "Let us do our work and wait for the right time." Mani nodded his head. Vetrivel went to clean the terrace, water tank, and solar panels. Then, in the early afternoon, Mani started to prepare the lunch, and Vetrivel tried his hands to fix the CCTV and DVX.

Arul drove back from Thanjavur at 2:00 p.m. with the medicines. Then he checked on Viji; he was glad to see that he had gained consciousness and strength, and he gave him some medicine and injections. "Don't worry, Viji. You are not in danger. You should thank God; the wounds are deep but missed the arteries and veins. You will walk soon." To Vetrivel, he said, "Where is Arivalagan?" Vetrivel replied, "He went around the village and surrounding areas." Then, he called Arivalagan over the phone. They waited for him, he rode in, and they all sat down for lunch. After having lunch, they sat down to discuss further plans.

Arul firmly said, "We will try our hands tonight. If we fail, we will inform the department and ask for support. This tiger is getting bolder. Anytime it further expands its area of operations, it will soon enter the village. What is your opinion, Arivalagan?" "That's what I thought. First, we should warn the villagers. I went around the village, and there were a lot of *Munthiri kaadu.* There is also another fish farm on the edge of the forest. People carelessly roam around, for they haven't seen a tiger for generations. I think the tiger is out of our hands. We should tell the department." Arul replied, "We will inform them tomorrow morning. What is our plan for tonight? Shall we make a human dummy and sit over it?" He turned to Vetrivel and asked, "Do you have any old dresses to make a dummy? I need pillows, thread, and needles, too."

Vetrivel brought the things Arul asked for. With old pants and shirts, pillows, and an old plastic ball from the children's room, Arul made a perfect dummy. He stitched the pants and shirt openings and stuffed the cotton from the pillows. He used the plastic ball, made it resemble a head, took a towel, and tied a *mundasu* around it to hide it. Then he looked at the dummy and thought for a while, "Do you have a white shirt and *vesti*? Let us recreate the Marthu scene. Tiger will remember successful kills and spots, so it's sure of taking the bait and giving a shot." "But you know the spot. There is no perfect place to hide. The house is also too far," reminded Arivalagan.

Arul said, "We will put the dummy near the bridge on the mud road. We will sit on the bridge. That path is often used and was also a successful spot." Arivalagan looked at him with doubt. "Should we both sit together? I am planning to sit on a tree on the way to the fish farm. There are a lot of people and activities in the early morning at the fish farm. What is your opinion?" Arul thought over it for a long time but eventually accepted it. Now, the dummy was ready. The *vesti* and white shirt from Vetrivel made the dummy look precisely like the village person.

Then they went to the bridge with their guns and sickles. Arul chose a spot 25 feet away from the bridge. They decided to sit under the bridge, facing the dummy. They cut the seemai karuvai branches and closed the other side of the bridge to avoid the tiger attacking from behind. They also cut down a few more thorns and shrubs nearby to cover their hide. Arivalagan got a four-foot-long stick and fastened it in the place marked for the dummy. They walked back to the house with all the work done to their satisfaction.

Arul and Arivalagan refreshed themselves and grabbed some snacks before returning to the bridge with the dummy. They planned to stay in their hideout throughout the night. After checking everything, Arul entered the bridge; Arivalagan secured and covered the opening of the bridge. Then Arivalagan tied the dummy to the stick and made it look like a man sitting and drinking liquor, which was a very common sight. He sat by the side of the dummy for some time and then walked out.

Since it was summer and the *agni natchathiram* was fast approaching, the bridge was very hot, and Arul started to sweat profusely. He checked his night scope and thermal binoculars. He opened the barrel of the gun and loaded a lethal ball on one barrel and a slug head on the other. He checked his rear and ensured there was no gap in the thorn enclosure. He kept everything within reach, took out his cell phone, and switched it off. After being fully satisfied with the arrangements made, he started to wait for the night and the tiger. He was very confident that the tiger would take the dummy and get shot.

Arivalagan went home, picked up Viji's rifle, and walked towards the fish farm. Unlike Arul and Viji, he always relied on his keen senses. He never used thermal scopes or binoculars. Despite repeated attempts at learning how to use them, he couldn't quite grasp it. He checked the rifle, cartridges, sickle, and rope and walked out. His mind had been warning him since morning, after the search for the tranquillised tiger, that the fish farm might be the next target.

As he neared the fish farm, he searched for a suitable tree to spend the night on it. Spotting a fig tree on the path, he made his way to it. The tree stood about twenty feet away from the road and had a large trunk with branches sprawling in all directions. He stood beneath the tree, scanning the surrounding shrubs and bushes for any signs of activity. He carefully selected a branch that would give him a perfect hide and a good view over the road and fish farm. He then dropped the bag and the rifle, tied them to one end of the rope, held the other end in his teeth, and climbed the tree. After climbing to a safe place, he pulled the rope up and got his rifle and bag. He started to look around and started his whole-night vigil.

Slowly, the evening vanished, and darkness fell around. It was a different situation from the forest that Arivalagan grew up in. In the forest where he grew up, there used to be a lot of animals and birds to warn of the approach and presence of a predator. But here, no such animals were there, only a few birds. And they, too, went silent after the darkness fell in. The only sound he heard around was the chirping of crickets. He started to wait, relying on his senses.

In the meantime, Arul was not comfortable in his hide. The time had passed around 10:00, but there was no sign of the tiger. He checked around the area with his thermal binoculars from time to time. He wondered whether the tiger had moved out to some other place. His confidence ran out.

NINETEEN

Unlike the previous Sundays, this Sunday was different for Pechimuthu and his family. The happenings in the family had made his heart heavy. Though they all lived as a joint family, they had differences of opinion under the carpet. Pechimuthu and his wife, Saroja, were the band that held the family together. Everything went well until their second son, Gokul, got married to Mathi. The family tried hard to cope with Mathi, but this morning, she shattered the family. A strange calmness and grief were prevailing in the family, and that could not be taken in and digested by Pechimuthu. So, he managed to escape that grim situation and took refuge in the *meen kuttai* he owned.

His family lived in Karuppukudi, and it was one of the few joint families left in the village. Pechimuthu and his wife Sarooja had three sons: Ganesh, Gokul, and Gopi; their family; and grandchildren. Their primary source of income was from the *meen kuttai*, the fish farm. The family never had a vast stretch of land of their own. They leased four acres of land with four big ponds and a bore well. They cultivated Katla, Rohu, Kendai, and Jalebi fish. The fish from their pond had a unique taste because they never used the company feed but *kadalai mavu*, *kadalai punnaku*, and *thavudu*.

Pechimuthu walked around the fence with his torchlight. He checked the ponds with his torch for fish gulping for oxygen on the surface and moved along the footpath between the ponds. The ponds were stretched in rows with a small strip of land mass in the centre, a bore well, and a big paran to accommodate four people.

The paran was constructed on stout bamboos at a height of 6 feet. The roof was made of *thenam keetru* and covered with tarpaulin. All four sides were left open but could be covered by tarpaulin sheets that were kept rolled up, with bamboo sticks tied to the edges to keep them in place when rolled down. It had a ladder to climb on the paran. It was the picnic spot for the family on the weekends and vacations.

Pechimuthu finished his rounds, climbed the ladder, reached the paran, and switched on the light. He cleaned the floor with a broom, stretched the mat and pillow, and sat on it. The incidents that happened in the morning unfolded in his mind.

Their first son, Ganesh, and his wife, Kani, were very supportive of the family's upbringing. But Mathi, the wife of Gokul, came from town and was more prosperous than the elder daughter-in-law. So, she was hesitant to do any help in fish farming or the chores at home. She was keen on splitting chores with her mother-in-law and sister-in-law. So, they both had to work in fishponds and come home to do the left out chores. Though they both grudged, they did the work silently. But after Gobi's marriage, matters worsened. The third daughter-in-law, Rekha, was very adamant about not going peacefully with Mathi. She also educated her mother-in-law and the elder sister-in-law not to go on terms with her. Every day became hell after that.

The weekdays were usually quiet for the brothers, but Sundays were always busy. On this day, most people buy non-vegetarian food, including fish. So, the brothers would prepare for Sunday sales by netting the fish the previous evening. The next day, early in the morning, they would load the fish onto their truck and deliver them to retailers as early as possible. Then they should run their retail fish shop. Ganesh would cut the fish, while Gokul, Gobi, and Pechimuthu would remove the fish scales and gills.

In the case of women, one of them will stay back, prepare breakfast and tea, and take care of the children. While the other women would help in the shop, weighing, cleaning, and maintaining cash. Mathi didn't like the smell of fish and the mess of cutting and cleaning, so she always preferred staying home and preparing breakfast. Fish sales would sometimes cross noon, and the urge for breakfast would be subsidised by several rounds of tea from home. Then, after finishing the sales, they would go home, bathe, have breakfast, and take a rest.

Gradually, Mathi's attitude changed a lot. She started behaving like she was the only one doing all the chores. She stopped preparing tea and sending it to the shop. Sometimes, the family would return from the shop and be disappointed to see that the breakfast was halfway through the preparation. She would tell them that the children kept her busy. One day, she bluntly told them she couldn't do chores and look after the children simultaneously. So, Saroja stayed back to help her. Even then, Saroja had to do all the work while she was busy with her mobile. Saroja didn't want to make it an issue and started to do all the work by herself.

Their house was not very big. So, when the house next to them was vacant and came up for rent, they leased it. Immediately, Mathi convinced her husband, made quite a scene, and moved into the newly leased house. Though they moved out, the kitchen was shared, and Gokul and his wife didn't cook separately. Gradually, her part in the cooking and helping with the chores completely stopped. But Saroja and Kani didn't mind it. Rekha watched these happenings and started open heated arguments with her.

This Sunday, as usual, the brothers went to the pond to load the fish for retailers and started business in their shop. Gokul told his brothers that he had some urgent work, left the shop, and never returned. When the family reached home, they were shocked that the breakfast was not ready; the children were playing alone, and Mathi was not seen. Their house was locked. Just then, Gokul entered with the parcel of idlis. When they all inquired about him, Gokul said that he and his wife had a severe quarrel the night before. In the heat of it, he ended up beating her. So, her father came in the morning, and she intended to leave without informing anyone in the family. But his father-in-law made a call secretly and informed Gokul. So, he came home to convince her. But she was adamant, and she left with her father. Then Gokul went to the shop and bought idlis for the children.

Pechimuthu lay down, worrying about the future of Gokul and his joint family. The day's hard work subsided his thoughts, and he slept for a while, forgetting all the incidents that happened in the morning. PLUP. The sound disturbed him. It's not new to him. It's the fish tossing out of the water. He heard it again, shortly followed by several thud sounds. He knew that the fish had jumped out and landed on the path between two ponds. It's usual, but it would be a disaster if the fish managed to move to the pond filled with the fries.

Though he felt sleepy, he had to check it. He reached out for the torch, grabbed it, and climbed down. The sound came from the south, so he walked in that direction, flashing the light. He walked to the end of the path and turned around. He could not find the fish. He was really worried, so he started scanning the path carefully. Within a few steps, he saw the wet ground. He searched around that place, but the fish was not found. But there were some footprints on the wet ground. He thought it must be a dog. He threw light in all directions and scanned the area. He decided to check it out in the morning.

He walked to the paran, climbed it, and settled on it. He lay down but couldn't sleep. The footprints flashed through his mind. The footprints were too big to be dogs. If it was a dog, then they should do something about it. His mind was haunted by thoughts. He felt something was wrong, and he felt uneasy. He sat up, leaning on the pole, his eyes gazing at the dark path before him. His eyes saw a movement on the side of the path; his whole body felt hot, and sweat started to pour out to cool it. He could not guess what it was. It was certainly too big for a dog. It resembled a cat, but was really very big. His hands reached the torch, and he threw light on it. The animal stopped. His eyes couldn't believe what he saw. For the first time in his life, he saw a tiger in person. He didn't know what to do.

He stood up, transfixed, looking at the tiger. With a loud growl, the tiger charged at him. He realised the danger, dropped the torch, and went near the pole, the edge of the paran. Should he jump into the water or climb on the roof of the paran? Before he could think, the tiger landed on the platform of the paran with a loud thud. He let out a cry. Every part of his body was trembling and sweating. Then, the tiger launched its final charge. Instinctively, his hand grabbed the pole above him and pulled his body up.

Despite his old age, he climbed the roof on time. The tiger missed him, fell into the fish pond, and started swimming around. He lay on the roof, holding tight. He was glad that he didn't jump into the pond. The tiger growled at him loudly. The noise was terrible and new to him. He held tightly to the roof and lay still. The tiger swam to the other side of the pond, jumped out of the water, shook its body, and ran.

Pechimutu was clinging to the roof desperately as his sweating body made the tarpaulin slippery. He held onto the ropes and bamboo crisscrossed to keep the tarpaulin in place while his body trembled from the shock caused by the tiger. Pechimutu stayed there for ten minutes until he was brought back to his senses by the sound of a motorcycle. He moved to the edge of the roof and saw the motorcycle heading towards the fish farm.

As the motorcycle entered the farm, he was relieved to see his son, Ganesh. However, a thought crossed his mind: if the tiger was still lurking around, it might attack him. So, he shouted to his son, "Ganesh, why did you come here? A tiger attacked me just now. It could be around here." Ganesh was startled by the voice of his father from the roof of the paran. He parked his bike and climbed the paran. He helped his father climb down. Ganesh said, "Appa, what happened? Why did you climb up there? The government has just announced a curfew in all the villages surrounding Karuppukudi. Many police and forest officials have arrived in our village. They are going street by street, announcing the tiger and urging us to stay indoors. I came to inform you of this situation and take you home."

Pechimuthu narrated the happenings, and Ganesh immediately called the *thaliyari* of the village and passed the matter. After fifteen minutes, a green Bolero came in, and the forest officials investigated the scene and took Pechimuthu and Ganesh with them.

TWENTY

Arivalagan heard the growling of the tiger and the screaming of a man, followed by the sound of a heavy object falling into the water from the fish farm. A swift coldness went through his body. His intuition was correct. The tiger had attacked the inhabitants of the lonely fish farm. Whether it succeeded in taking a kill was not known to him. He strained his eyes and ears into the darkness to locate the tiger's movement. The stars had appeared in the sky and gave a dim light around. The growl and the screaming made the entire area fall silent. The chirping had stopped and warned him that the tiger was still in the vicinity. His eyes searched the bushes and the shadows for any movement. Finally, after a few minutes, he heard an animal moving through the bushes. He assumed the direction and scanned the darkness for any movement. The sound told him that the animal was moving slowly and steadily. If it had secured a kill, it would move fast, like a thief. But the phase was slow and regular. His eyes spotted a dark object moving in the shades of the bushes, but the distance was far, so he waited to get closer to him. It was the tiger, for sure; it was not in a hurry and not carrying any victim. Arivalagan heaved a sigh of relief, as the tiger had not secured a kill and was now moving away at a normal pace. He wondered what the tiger's next move would be. Would it fall for the dummy bait and give Arul a chance to kill it, or would it attack a lone rider on the road or enter the village?

Unexpectedly, the tiger changed its direction and came towards the tree where Arivalagan was sitting. Arivalagan realised it and got ready. He sat out patiently till the tiger came close to the tree. When it was twenty feet away from the tree, Arivalagan brought the butt of the rifle to the shoulder and switched on the torch attached to the rifle barrel. The bright light stunned the tiger, and it stopped for a few seconds. It was walking in the cover of the bushes. Hunger and tiredness were visible on its face. Water was dripping, its face was gutted in several places, and one eye shone brightly in the torchlight while the other was just dark. The wounds in the face had damaged the eyesight. Arul aligned the sight and pressed the trigger. Instead of a loud bang, the rifle clicked, and the cartridge misfired. Before he pressed the trigger of the second barrel, the tiger sensed the danger and vanished. Arul then unloaded the misfired cartridge and loaded a new one. However, he was now more concerned about the rifle than the tiger. He wondered whether the cartridge or the rifle was at fault and how he could test it.

Based on his experience, he knew that the tiger would not leave anytime soon. It would likely be waiting nearby, ready to pounce if he carelessly descended the tree. Additionally, he was worried about the condition of his rifle. He decided to stay in the tree for a while to be safe. He shone the torch around and carefully scanned the bushes and branches for any sign of movement, but he couldn't spot the tiger. Frustrated, he turned off the light and sat still, hoping to avoid detection. Arivalagan cursed his misfortune, the tiger's luck, and the cartridge that failed to fire. He closed his eyes and listened intently for any sign of movement. He remained motionless for some time. Then he heard the engine sound of a jeep from the *meen kuttai.* He understood that the person must have called in for help, and now the matter is out of his hands. The crickets chirped after a while, indicating that the tiger had moved away from the area.

Arivalagan realised that staying on the tree wouldn't serve any purpose. Therefore, he decided to spend the night sitting on a tree near the road or at the school building. This way, he could protect people passing by from any potential attacks. Moreover, now that the villagers knew the presence of the tiger, he wanted to convey it to Arul and discuss the next move. If they had to leave, they should do it now.

He tied his rifle and bag to the rope and slowly lowered them to the ground. After ensuring that everything was secure, he carefully climbed down and touched the ground. Quickly grabbed the rifle, leaned onto the trunk of the tree, brought the rifle butt to his shoulder, and looked around. His previous experience in the forest told him that the tiger had left the area. But this tiger had a peculiar way of waiting in the distance, even after a shot. So, he decided not to give up his precautions. If he switched on the torch, it would attract the tiger, so he moved in the darkness with his rifle butt to his shoulders and inched his way, looking around carefully.

Meanwhile, under the bridge, Arul was losing his patience. His plan to use a dummy had failed miserably. The dummy he had used had also collapsed. The ball he had used as the head had fallen out of its place, and the rope tied to the stick had either broken or loosened. Consequently, the head appeared to be bent over the dummy's knees. Despite the setback, he had no other options, so he decided to wait until the morning.

In the morning, he planned to make a call to the forest department and make a complaint in the name of Vetrivel, and then, using Viji's condition, he and Arivalagan would escape the scene before the police and forest officials came in. He took out his thermal binoculars and looked around. He saw the red image of a man walking, looking around with something like a rifle. He immediately understood that it was Arivalagan and that he was walking towards him, expecting an attack from the tiger. He looked around carefully in all directions through the binoculars. The tiger was not anywhere without knowing that Arivalagan was taking all precautions. Arul laughed at his behaviour in his mind. He had taught him several times to use thermal imagers. But he was not learning it. He wondered why Arivalagan gave up his position. Arul could not take it anymore. So, he decided to get out of his hide under the bridge and join him. He gathered his equipment, used his rifle butt to push off the thorn enclosure, and came out.

As he stood up and levelled the bridge, he heard a deep growl from behind, over the bridge. When he turned around, he saw the tiger crouching on its haunches. Quickly, he raised his rifle to his shoulder, but the tiger pounced on him. He threw himself back and hastily pulled the trigger. The tiger landed on him; its claws mauled his shoulders, and he cried in pain. Arivalagan heard the gunshot and cries and came running to the spot. He helped Arul sit up. "What happened? Why the hell did you come out of the hide?" shouted Arivalagan. Arul replied, "Stop talking and watch out for the tiger. You know what it did after attacking Viji. Arul took out his medical kit and attended to his wounds. Then he started explaining his encounter with the tiger. "You were looking for the tiger while it was sitting right above you." Arivalagan laughed. "Again, it was a clear miss at point-blank range. Strange, isn't it? Either the tiger is lucky, or we have lost our hunting skills," said Arivalagan. Arul nodded his head.

Arul's bleeding stopped. He took out his binoculars and looked around. "It's not around here," Arul said. Arivalagan switched on the torch of his rifle and checked the ground in the direction the tiger went. "Look here. Blood trail; you had wounded it. The trail shows the wound is big." Arul gathered his things. "That's the reason it didn't come back." They walked along the trail, and the trail ran into the seemai karuvai Kadu, where Viji was attacked. They stopped there. "It's dangerous to go in," said Arivalagan. Arul nodded his head. Then they walked towards the house. When they entered the gate, they could see Vetrivel and Mani waiting for them at the gates. "We heard the sound of the gun. What happened?" asked Vetrivel. "First, let's go inside," said Arivalagan. Both climbed the stairs and reached the house. Arul settled in the first room on the first floor, along with Viji. Viji got upset. "What happened?" Arul explained everything in detail. "The tiger is getting more cunning," said Viji. "No, the tiger was stalking and was about to attack the dummy. Arul came onto the scene and got attacked. I have told you several times about the patience needed in hunting. If you had stayed in the hide, it would have attacked the dummy and given you a clean shot." Then, Arivalagan narrated his part of the encounter with the tiger and the misfire. Arul gazed into the eyes of Arivalagan when he told about the sound of the jeep he heard in *meen kuttai*. Arul looked at his wounds and said to Arivalagan, "My wounds are deep and look serious. We must get to the nearest hospital. Let me finish the first-aid, and then we can go."

Arivalagan helped Arul clean the wounds. Bandages were running short. Arul said, "Arivalagan, bring all the things available in the medical kit from the Jeep. We can't run down often to get the supplies." Arul was glad that he had bought all the essential supplies in the morning. Arivalagan opened the door and went down with a bag.

Vetrivel posed as though he couldn't withstand the blood and wounds, and he walked out of the room after hearing the happenings. But in his mind, he was contemplating a way to contact his friend at the police. Mani stayed with them and helped them. Vetrivel saw Arivalagan rushing out. He walked to the hall, switched on the TV, and started watching the CCTV feed he had fixed in the morning. He saw Arivalagan going near the Jeep and selected all the ground floor cameras. The ground floor had four colour night vision IP cameras, and the feed came into view, covering the compounds and gate.

Vetrivel's eyes were fixed on the rear compound wall. He selected that camera, and the feed came into full screen. He saw red-coloured patches on the compound wall and traces on the floor. He remembered that Arul shot and wounded the tiger and that the tiger left a blood trail. Before he warned others, things started to happen.

In the parking area, Arivalagan opened the door of the Jeep and started taking the bandages, the cotton, and other medicines. Suddenly, he felt something hit his legs hard, and he fell like a tree cut down. His back hurt, and he cried in pain. Then something grabbed his leg and pulled him under the Jeep. Only then did he realise it was the tiger and hold on to the running board of the jeep. He screamed in pain. Vetrivel heard him and rushed down, shouting, "Tiger!" Mani followed him. They saw Arivalagan holding the running board of the jeep firmly and crying in agony.

Vetrivel and Mani grabbed Arivalagan's shoulder and pulled him. Arivalagan cried in pain. Both pulled Arivalagan from the teeth of the tiger. His left leg was torn to strips. He cried in pain. Vetrivel said, "You bring Arul to the balcony. From there, he can shoot the tiger. I will help Arivalagan." While Main rushed up the stairs, Vetrivel helped Arivalagan get on his feet. And then the tiger jumped on the bonnet of the jeep. It landed with a groan. It was bleeding on the right hind leg. It growled at them with hatred, and the sound was dreadful.

Vetrivel saw the tiger for the first time, so close to him. The appearance of the tiger was shocking to him. His reflexes had failed, and he stood still. With shivering and sweat running all over his body, he stood looking at it motionless. Arivalagan pushed Vetrivel, shouted, "Run," fell, and pulled himself under the jeep since he couldn't stand. Vetrivel turned and ran up the stairs. The tiger jumped on Vetrivel and landed on his back with a loud growl. Vetrivel pushed it with all his strength. The tiger lost its balance and tumbled down the stairs. Vetrivel fell on the stairs; his nose started to bleed, and his back was torn and bleeding from the wounds made by the claws. Before the tiger stood on its legs, Vetrivel gathered himself, ran upstairs, entered the first room, and locked the door behind him. Arivalagan had managed to enter the Jeep through the driver's door and lock it. The tiger went around the Jeep several times, then climbed upstairs. When it almost entered the house, he heard the window of the room being opened. Arivalagan shouted to his friends, "I am safe. The tiger is inside the house; don't open the door." Inside the room, everyone huddled behind the closed door. Arul signalled them to be silent.

Arivalagan was reminded of how Vetrivel and his family trapped the dacoits. He slowly opened the door of the Jeep and started climbing upstairs, holding the rails and dragging his wounded legs. He was bleeding and sweating profoundly. Meanwhile, the tiger started clawing at the door of the room.

Arivalagan reached the gate and locked it. He started shouting and beating the gate. The tiger heard the sound, rushed out, saw Arivalagan, and growled at him. It tried to claw him through the gate. Arivalagan shouted in his full throat, "Come out and close the door. The tiger is outside the house.".

Vetrivel opened the door slowly and looked around through the narrow opening. Arivalagan again shouted, "Do it fast." Mani moved Vetrivel aside, ran to the front door, and locked it. Now, the tiger was trapped on the balcony. It heard the door, ran towards it, and clawed it vigorously. The door almost got dislodged. Vetrivel shouted to Mani, "Close the safety gate. Let us not take chances." Mani locked the safety door and felt relieved that they were safe at last. The tiger went back to Arivalagan and growled at him. He could feel the thrust of the tiger on the door and grill.

Arivalagan couldn't stand it anymore. He sat on the stairs and almost slid downstairs. He reached the Jeep, climbed inside, and closed the door. He could still hear the tiger's thrust on the grill and the door. Its growling was thundering and gave shock waves all over his body. He hoped that the gate would hold.

After relaxing for a few minutes, Mani slipped through the backdoor, brought down the ladder from the terrace, laid it on the ground floor, and climbed down it. He hurriedly reached Arivalagan. Then he heard the thunderous roar from the tiger. He turned around and looked at it. The tiger was barring its deadly teeth, with blood dripping from the mouth and hair. With hate and power, the tiger was ragging the gate. It was the most horrifying scene of his life. Arivalagan was almost exhausted and was about to faint. If he faints, taking him to the room would be difficult. He opened the door of the Jeep, helped him get down, and walked him to the ladder. Vetrivel and Arul were waiting upstairs.

Arivalagan, with great difficulty, climbed the ladder with one leg. Mani followed him, holding him back from falling. After reaching the room, Arul treated Vetrivel and Arivalagan with the medical kit and stopped their bleeding. Arivalagan had deep wounds, and he needed immediate medical assistance. Arul gave Vetrivel his phone and asked him to call everyone: ambulances, police, villagers, and the forest department. Arul now knew that everyone in his team was wounded and that an escape would be impossible. Arivalagan's condition was very bad, so he decided to stay and face the consequences.

Vetrivel called his friend in the police department and then informed the friends in the village and explained the situation. After Vetrivel finished his call, Arul made a few calls to his friends in higher positions. Then he attended to the wounds of Vetrivel and Arivalagan. The police and the forest department came in ten minutes, for they were waiting for his call in Karuppukudi. Ambulances were brought in, and Arivalagan, Arul, and Viji were dispatched to the Medical College hospital in Thanjavur. Vetrivel's wound was not severe, and first-aid was sufficient for him, so he stayed back. Mani, too, stayed with him. Within half an hour, the whole village gathered near the house. They were pretty shocked to see the bloody scene and the angry tiger.

When the situation eased, Vetrivel approached his friend in the police department and asked, "Will Arul, Viji, and Arivalagan be arrested after their treatment?" The officer replied, "Those persons have contacts in high positions. When we first informed the forest department, they said they didn't know them. Now they say that they were working here at the request of the forest department. So, nothing could be done."

Meanwhile, the veterinary doctors sedated the tiger, started treating the gun wound, and transported it to Thanjavur. The police and the forest department finished their formalities and left the place. Vetrivel and Mani started to wait for their families. The news was spread in the media. Once again, the house gained prominence in the news.

The government announced compensation for the victims. Arul and Viji recovered from their injuries. Arivalagan lost his foot but recovered. They, too, received their part of the compensation and started a new life.

Ilakiyaa's family grieved the brutal death of their daughter. To say the least, they were happy that the defamed image of the girl had been restored. Muthu's family received compensation from the government and the cement company, and his wife was offered a job in the factory office. Soundar's wife grieved over the death of her husband, but his son was not moved; he felt that he deserved it.

After a few weeks, Vetrivel and Vairavel's families arrived for their vacation and spent a month at the house. During their stay, they discussed plans to further fortify the property. As part of these plans, Mathialagan was hired as the new caretaker of the farm and was given the newly constructed house on the third floor. Vetrivel moved back to Valluvar Illam, with his family and started the fortification work. The fence was removed, a ten-foot-high compound wall was constructed, and the barbed wire was installed on top of it. Cameras and lights were installed along the compound wall. A mighty gate and a new name stone welcomed the visitors; with the name Valluvar Illam in small letters and in bold letters, it read, KASAN KADU.

THE END

www.ingramcontent.com/pod-product-compliance
Lightning Source LLC
LaVergne TN
LVHW041220150826
845673LV00001B/465

* 9 7 9 8 8 9 1 8 6 9 9 1 2 *